Hell Squad: Marcus

Anna Hackett

Marcus

Published by Anna Hackett

Cover by Melody Simmons of eBookindiecovers
Edits by Tanya Saari

ISBN (eBook): 978-0-9941948-3-1
ISBN (paperback): 978-0-9941948-7-9

What readers are saying about Anna's Science Fiction Romance

At Star's End - One of Library Journal's Best E-Original Romances for 2014

The Phoenix Adventures – SFR Galaxy Award winner for Most Fun New Series

The Anomaly Series – An Action Adventure Romance Bestseller

"Action, danger, aliens, romance – yup, it's another great book from Anna Hackett!" – Book Gannet Reviews, review of *Hell Squad: Marcus*

"Action, adventure, heartache and hot steamy love scenes." – Amazon reviewer, review of *Hell Squad: Cruz*

"Hell Squad is a terrific series. Each book is a sexy, fast-paced adventure guaranteed to please." – Amazon reviewer, review of *Hell Squad: Gabe*

Don't miss out! For updates about new releases, action romance info, free books, and other fun stuff, sign up for my VIP mailing list and get your free copy of the Phoenix Adventures novella, *On a Cyborg Planet.*

Visit here to get started:
www.annahackettbooks.com

Chapter One

Her team was under attack.

Elle Milton pressed her fingers to her small earpiece. "Squad Six, you have seven more raptors inbound from the east." Her other hand gripped the edge of her comp screen, showing the enhanced drone feed.

She watched, her belly tight, as seven glowing red dots converged on the blue ones huddled together in the burned-out ruin of an office building in downtown Sydney. Each blue dot was a squad member and one of them was their leader.

"Marcus? Do you copy?" Elle fought to keep her voice calm. No way she'd let them hear her alarm.

"Roger that, Elle." Marcus' gravelly voice filled her ear. Along with the roar of laser fire. "We see them."

She sagged back in her chair. This was the worst part. Just sitting there knowing that Marcus and the others were fighting for their lives. In the six months she'd been comms officer for the squad, she'd worked hard to learn the ropes. But there were days she wished she was out there, aiming a gun and taking out as many alien raptors as she could.

You're not a soldier, Ellianna. No, she was a useless party-girl-turned-survivor. She watched as a red dot disappeared off the screen, then another, and another. She finally drew a breath. Marcus and his team were the experienced soldiers. She'd just be a big fat liability in the field.

But she was a damn good comms officer.

Just then, a new cluster of red dots appeared near the team. She tapped the screen, took a measurement. "Marcus! More raptors are en route. They're about one kilometer away. North." God, would these invading aliens ever leave them alone?

"Shit," Marcus bit out. Then he went silent.

She didn't know if he was thinking or fighting. She pictured his rugged, scarred face creased in thought as he formulated a plan.

Then his deep, rasping voice was back. "Elle, we need an escape route and an evac now. Shaw's been hit in the leg, Cruz is carrying him. We can't engage more raptors."

She tapped the screen rapidly, pulling up drone images and archived maps. *Escape route, escape route.* Her mind clicked through the options. She knew Shaw was taller and heavier than Cruz, but the armor they wore had slim-line exoskeletons built into them allowing the soldiers to lift heavier loads and run faster and longer than normal. She tapped the screen again. *Come on.* She needed somewhere safe for a Hawk quadcopter to set down and pick them up.

"Elle? We need it now!"

Just then her comp beeped. She looked at the

image and saw a hazy patch of red appear in the broken shell of a nearby building. The heat sensor had detected something else down there. Something big.

Right next to the team.

She touched her ear. "Rex! Marcus, a rex has just woken up in the building beside you."

"Fuck! Get us out of here. Now."

Oh, God. Elle swallowed back bile. Images of rexes, with their huge, dinosaur-like bodies and mouths full of teeth, flashed in her head.

More laser fire ripped through her earpiece and she heard the wild roar of the awakening beast.

Block it out. She focused on the screen. Marcus needed her. The team needed her.

"Run past the rex." One hand curled into a tight fist, her nails cutting into her skin. "Go through its hiding place."

"Through its nest?" Marcus' voice was incredulous. "You know how territorial they are."

"It's the best way out. On the other side you'll find a railway tunnel. Head south along it about eight hundred meters, and you'll find an emergency exit ladder that you can take to the surface. I'll have a Hawk pick you up there."

A harsh expulsion of breath. "Okay, Elle. You've gotten us out of too many tight spots for me to doubt you now."

His words had heat creeping into her cheeks. His praise...it left her giddy. In her life BAI—before alien invasion—no one had valued her opinions. Her father, her mother, even her almost-fiancé, they'd all thought her nothing more than a pretty ornament. Hell, she *had* been a silly, pretty party girl.

And because she'd been inept, her parents were dead. Elle swallowed. A year had passed since that horrible night during the first wave of the alien attack, when their giant ships had appeared in the skies. Her parents had died that night, along with most of the world.

"Hell Squad, ready to go to hell?" Marcus called out.

"Hell, yeah!" the team responded. "The devil needs an ass-kicking!"

"Woo-hoo!" Another voice blasted through her headset, pulling her from the past. "Ellie, baby, this dirty alien's nest stinks like Cruz's socks. You should be here."

A smile tugged at Elle's lips. Shaw Baird always knew how to ease the tension of a life-or-death situation.

"Oh, yeah, Hell Squad gets the best missions," Shaw added.

Elle watched the screen, her smile slipping. Everyone called Squad Six the Hell Squad. She was never quite sure if it was because they were hellions, or because they got sent into hell to do the toughest, dirtiest missions.

There was no doubt they were a bunch of rebels. Marcus had a rep for not following orders. Just the previous week, he'd led the squad in to destroy a raptor outpost but had detoured to rescue survivors huddled in an abandoned hospital that was under attack. At the debrief, the general's yelling had echoed through the entire base. Marcus, as always, had been silent.

"Shut up, Shaw, you moron." The deep female voice carried an edge.

Elle had decided there were two words that best described the only female soldier on Hell Squad—loner and tough. Claudia Frost was everything Elle wasn't. Elle cleared her throat. "Just get yourselves back to base."

As she listened to the team fight their way through the rex nest, she tapped in the command for one of the Hawk quadcopters to pick them up.

The line crackled. "Okay, Elle, we're through. Heading to the evac point."

Marcus' deep voice flowed over her and the tense muscles in her shoulders relaxed a fraction. They'd be back soon. They were okay. He was okay.

She pressed a finger to the blue dot leading the team. "The bird's en route, Marcus."

"Thanks. See you soon."

She watched on the screen as the large, black shadow of the Hawk hovered above the ground and the team boarded. The rex was headed in their direction, but they were already in the air.

Elle stood and ran her hands down her trousers. She shot a wry smile at the camouflage fabric. It felt like a dream to think that she'd ever owned a very expensive, designer wardrobe. And heels—God, how long had it been since she'd worn heels? These days, fatigues were all that hung in her closet. Well-worn ones, at that.

As she headed through the tunnels of the underground base toward the landing pads, she forced herself not to run. She'd see him—them—soon enough. She rounded a corner and almost collided with someone.

"General. Sorry, I wasn't watching where I was going."

"No problem, Elle." General Adam Holmes had a military-straight bearing he'd developed in the United Coalition Army and a head of dark hair with a brush of distinguished gray at his temples. He was classically handsome, and his eyes were a piercing blue. He was the top man in this last little outpost of humanity. "Squad Six on their way back?"

"Yes, sir." They fell into step.

"And they secured the map?"

God, Elle had almost forgotten about the map. "Ah, yes. They got images of it just before they came under attack by raptors."

"Well, let's go welcome them home. That map might just be the key to the fate of mankind."

They stepped into the landing areas. Staff in various military uniforms and civilian clothes raced around. After the raptors had attacked, bringing all manner of vicious creatures with them to take over the Earth, what was left of mankind had banded together.

Whoever had survived now lived here in an underground base in the Blue Mountains, just west of Sydney, or in the other, similar outposts scattered across the planet. All arms of the United

Coalition's military had been decimated. In the early days, many of the surviving soldiers had fought amongst themselves, trying to work out who outranked whom. But it didn't take long before General Holmes had unified everyone against the aliens. Most squads were a mix of ranks and experience, but the teams eventually worked themselves out. Most didn't even bother with titles and rank anymore.

Sirens blared, followed by the clang of metal. Huge doors overhead retracted into the roof.

A Hawk filled the opening, with its sleek gray body and four spinning rotors. It was near-silent, running on a small thermonuclear engine. It turned slowly as it descended to the landing pad.

Her team was home.

She threaded her hands together, her heart beating a little faster.

Marcus was home.

***

Marcus Steele wanted a shower and a beer.

Hot, sweaty and covered in raptor blood, he leaped down from the Hawk and waved at his team to follow. He kept a sharp eye on the medical team who raced out to tend to Shaw. Dr. Emerson Green was leading them, her white lab coat snapping around her curvy body. The blonde doctor caught his gaze and tossed him a salute.

Shaw was cursing and waving them off, but one look from Marcus and the lanky Australian sniper shut his mouth.

Marcus swung his laser carbine over his shoulder and scraped a hand down his face. Man, he'd kill for a hot shower. Of course, he'd have to settle for a cold one since they only allowed hot water for two hours in the morning in order to conserve energy. But maybe after that beer he'd feel human again.

"Well done, Squad Six." Holmes stepped forward. "Steele, I hear you got images of the map."

Holmes might piss Marcus off sometimes, but at least the guy always got straight to the point. He was a general to the bone and always looked spit and polish. Everything about him screamed money and a fancy education, so not surprisingly, he tended to rub the troops the wrong way.

Marcus pulled the small, clear comp chip from his pocket. "We got it."

Then he spotted her.

Shit. It was always a small kick in his chest. His gaze traveled up Elle Milton's slim figure, coming to rest on a face he could stare at all day. She wasn't very tall, but that didn't matter. Something about her high cheekbones, pale-blue eyes, full lips, and rain of chocolate-brown hair…it all worked for him. Perfectly. She was beautiful, kind, and far too good to be stuck in this crappy underground maze of tunnels, dressed in hand-me-down fatigues.

She raised a slim hand. Marcus shot her a small nod.

"Hey, Ellie-girl. Gonna give me a kiss?"

Shaw passed on an iono-stretcher hovering off

the ground and Marcus gritted his teeth. The tall, blond sniper with his lazy charm and Aussie drawl was popular with the ladies. Shaw flashed his killer smile at Elle.

She smiled back, her blue eyes twinkling and Marcus' gut cramped.

Then she put one hand on her hip and gave the sniper a head-to-toe look. She shook her head. "I think you get enough kisses."

Marcus released the breath he didn't realize he was holding.

"See you later, Sarge." Zeke Jackson slapped Marcus on the back and strolled past. His usually-silent twin, Gabe, was beside him. The twins, both former Coalition Army Special Forces soldiers, were deadly in the field. Marcus was damned happy to have them on his squad.

"Howdy, Princess." Claudia shot Elle a smirk as she passed.

Elle rolled her eyes. "Claudia."

Cruz, Marcus' second-in-command and best friend from their days as Coalition Marines, stepped up beside Marcus and crossed his arms over his chest. He'd already pulled some of his lightweight body armor off, and the ink on his arms was on display.

The general nodded at Cruz before looking back at Marcus. "We need Shaw back up and running ASAP. If the raptor prisoner we interrogated is correct, that map shows one of the main raptor communications hubs." There was a blaze of excitement in the usually-stoic general's voice. "It links all their operations together."

Yeah, Marcus knew it was big. Destroy the hub, send the raptor operations into disarray.

The general continued. "As soon as the tech team can break the encryption on the chip and give us a location for the raptor comms hub—" his piercing gaze leveled on Marcus "—I want your team back out there to plant the bomb."

Marcus nodded. He knew if they destroyed the raptors' communications it gave humanity a fighting chance. A chance they desperately needed.

He traded a look with Cruz. Looked like they were going out to wade through raptor gore again sooner than anticipated.

Man, he really wanted that beer.

Then Marcus' gaze landed on Elle again. He didn't keep going out there for himself, or Holmes. He went so people like Elle and the other civilian survivors had a chance. A chance to do more than simply survive.

"Shaw's wound is minor. Doc Emerson should have him good as new in an hour or so." Since the advent of the nano-meds, simple wounds could be healed in hours, rather than days and weeks. They carried a dose of the microscopic medical machines on every mission, but only for dire emergencies. The nano-meds had to be administered and monitored by professionals or they were just as likely to kill you from the inside than heal you.

General Holmes nodded. "Good."

Elle cleared her throat. "There's no telling how long it will take to break the encryption. I've been working with the tech team and even if they break it, we may not be able to translate it all. We're getting better at learning the raptor language but there are still huge amounts of it we don't yet understand."

Marcus' jaw tightened. There was always something. He knew Noah Kim—their resident genius computer specialist—and his geeks were good, but if they couldn't read the damn raptor language…

Holmes turned. "Steele, let your team have some downtime and be ready the minute Noah has anything."

"Yes, sir." As the general left, Marcus turned to Cruz. "Go get yourself a beer, Ramos."

"Don't need to tell me more than once, *amigo*. I would kill for some of my dad's tamales to go with it." Something sad flashed across a face all the women in the base mooned over, then he grimaced and a bone-deep weariness colored his words. "Need to wash the raptor off me, first." He tossed Marcus a casual salute, Elle a smile, and strode out.

Marcus frowned after his friend and absently started loosening his body armor.

Elle moved up beside him. "I can take the comp chip to Noah."

"Sure." He handed it to her. When her fingers brushed his he felt the warmth all the way through him. Hell, he had it bad. Thankfully, he still had his armor on or she'd see his cock tenting his pants.

"I'll come find you as soon as we have

something." She glanced up at him. Smiled. "Are you going to rec night tonight? I hear Cruz might even play guitar for us."

The Friday-night gathering was a chance for everyone to blow off a bit of steam and drink too much homebrewed beer. And Cruz had an unreal talent with a guitar, although lately Marcus hadn't seen the man play too much.

Marcus usually made an appearance at these parties, then left early to head back to his room to study raptor movements or plan the squad's next missions. "Yeah, I'll be there."

"Great." She smiled. "I'll see you there, then." She hurried out clutching the chip.

He stared at the tunnel where she'd exited for a long while after she disappeared, and finally ripped his chest armor off. Ah, on second thought, maybe going to the rec night wasn't a great idea. Watching her pretty face and captivating smile would drive him crazy. He cursed under his breath. He really needed that cold shower.

As he left the landing pads, he reminded himself he should be thinking of the mission. Destroy the hub and kill more aliens. Rinse and repeat. Death and killing, that was about all he knew.

He breathed in and caught a faint trace of Elle's floral scent. She was clean and fresh and good. She always worried about them, always had a smile, and she was damned good at providing their comms and intel.

She was why he fought through the muck every day. So she could live and the goodness in her would survive. She deserved more than blood and death and killing.

And she sure as hell deserved more than a battled-scarred, bloodstained soldier.

Chapter Two

"What do you mean you haven't got anything off the chip?" Elle stared at Noah Kim, unable to take in what he'd just told her.

Noah sat back in his chair, surrounded by a mess of salvaged, mismatched computer equipment in the computer lab. A lab he considered his own private domain. He rolled something around in his left hand and Elle knew it would be a pair of dice from his collection.

"I got the data off the chip, Ellie, it's just undecipherable."

No. She gripped the edge of the table. Marcus and others were *not* going to be happy.

Noah pushed his dark-rimmed glasses up his nose. He was long and lean with a handsome face dominated by high cheekbones and dark eyes courtesy of his South Korean father. His black hair was in desperate need of a cut and brushed his shoulders.

"There are too many new letters and words. You've been working on the raptor language project, you know we can only translate a small portion of it."

Elle released a breath. Yes, she knew and Noah

never lied. He always gave people the stark truth whether they wanted it or not. "Dammit."

He patted her hand. "Sorry. I know it wasn't what you wanted to hear."

"You'll keep working on it?"

"You know I will." He leaned back and set his dice on the shelf behind him. On it, lined up with precision, was his collection—dice of all shapes, sizes and colors. Some were ancient and made from bone, others were electronic and made of metal. The man was obsessed and didn't let anyone touch them, ever.

Back at his desk, he picked up what looked like…well, she had no idea what the mass of chips and wires was. "I have some priority work to do on the solar-power system, then I'll get to it. Promise."

A hundred years before, some genius had perfected making nuclear power safe. But only on a small scale. Tiny thermonuclear reactors could power a quadcopter or a vehicle, but something as large as Blue Mountain Base couldn't be powered by them. They'd just end up with more nuclear waste than they could neutralize. Instead, they relied on a high-tech solar-power system that Noah kept running.

She nodded. "Well, I'll go and tell Squad Six the bad news."

He winced. "I don't envy you the task of telling Hell Squad they just risked their butts for nothing."

"They're used to risking their lives." Too much, in her opinion. "And it isn't for nothing. We *will* find a way to translate that map, or we might all end up raptor bait."

Elle hit the tunnel and headed toward the rec room.

Over the last year, the bare concrete walls and twisting tunnels had become familiar. The polished wood and luxury furniture of her parents' sprawling mansion seemed a distant dream. As she neared the large open space that had become the recreation area, she heard the strum of strings and the murmur of conversation punctuated by the odd laugh.

She paused in the arched doorway. It was busy tonight. It seemed like most of the base was packed into the room, leaning against the walls and lounging on chairs. A slim man was playing guitar, bent over the battered instrument, lost in his music. A couple of women in tight jeans had gamely cleared a small space near him and were dancing.

Elle spotted the members of Six by the far wall. Shaw—newly healed—straddled a chair backwards, the light glinting off the golden strands in his hair. He was laughing at something the intense, tall and imposing Gabe had said. Gabe, with his shaved head, dark skin and tattoos, didn't appear to notice that many people detoured around him to avoid gaining his attention.

Claudia was sitting cross-legged on top of a table, swigging back a beer, her dark hair in its usual braid. Marcus and Cruz leaned against the wall. Only Zeke, Gabe's twin brother, was missing.

Her gaze instantly went to Marcus, drawn there like metal to a magnet. Her breath hitched. He'd showered, his short, dark hair damp against his head. He wore a well-worn, black T-shirt and even more well-worn jeans that were going threadbare at the stress points. Marcus wasn't the tallest member of his team, but he was the biggest. He had a tough, solid body that was all muscle. His arms were crossed, his biceps bulging, a beer dangling from his fingers. He was listening to something Cruz was saying.

Elle bit her lip. Every single cell in her body vibrated with need. She'd never, ever wanted a man so much. She had no idea why he affected her so much. Cruz, with his liquid-dark eyes, mouthwatering face and a sexy Latin accent, was more handsome. Most women in the base were half in love with Cruz's trademark sexy grin. Elle had heard one woman call it panty-melting, but it didn't have that effect on Elle.

Marcus' face was rough, tough, and dominated by a large, ragged scar that ran down his right cheek and across his neck. No one knew how he'd gotten it. Rumor said he'd charged a raptor raiding party in the early days after the invasion. That he'd killed them all with his bare hands and been given a slash during the fight for his trouble.

Elle had no idea if it was true, but she had no trouble believing he could do it.

As she watched, Claudia said something that had a small smile curving his lips. Elle's shoulders sagged. Claudia was so his type—a strong, female warrior. Never in a million years would he want a woman like Elle. The thought left a bitter taste in her mouth.

"Hey, Elle. Want a beer?"

She blinked and focused on the man just inside the door, manning the makeshift bar. "Ah, no thanks, Zeke."

It would be easy to mistake Zeke for simply a bartender and not the soldier he was. With his brightly colored Hawaiian shirt, cargo shorts, and dark skin topped with a lazy smile, he didn't look like a man who could battle through raptors with focused ease.

Zeke waved a hand behind him. "The best homebrewed beer in Blue Mountain Base. Or if you want to go all out, the last of the top-shelf liquor." He pointed to the mostly empty spirit bottles lining the shelves behind him.

"Another time. I need to talk to Marcus."

Zeke frowned. "Bad news?"

"Something like that." Elle wove through the crowd, responding when required to hellos and calls to join groups for a drink.

She was almost to Marcus when she saw a tall, curvaceous blonde saunter up to him.

Liberty was beautiful and she knew how to work it. Considering the world had gone to hell, the woman spent a long time ensuring her mane of hair stayed healthy and blonde. Elle had heard Liberty had started an underground black market in scavenged beauty products. She packed her curves into tight jeans and a shirt the color of strawberries that showed off her assets.

Elle liked her. She was funny and unapologetic about the fact she liked sex. With well-muscled soldiers. The harder and sweatier the better. Some of her stories made Elle blush.

But as the woman sidled up beside Marcus, a flirtatious grin on her face, all of Elle's kind feelings toward the other woman evaporated. Suddenly, all Elle wanted to do was leap on her and take her down.

Elle forced herself to breathe. If Marcus wanted to spend the night tangled with Liberty, it was none of her business.

So why the hell did she feel like she was bleeding inside?

Liberty pressed up close to Marcus, her breasts rubbing against his arm. She said something and Marcus responded. Elle secretly liked the fact his face stayed its usual impassive mask.

Liberty finally nodded and walked away. She blew Marcus a kiss over her shoulder.

Had they made plans to meet later? Elle forced her feet to move. *None of your damn business, Elle.*

She stiffened her spine and hoped the look on her face was cool and professional.

***

"You should take her up on her offer, *amigo*. She's a fast, sweaty ride to heaven."

Marcus grunted at Cruz's words. "Not interested."

Since the alien invasion, most people's views on sex had changed. Sex was a way to affirm life, feel closeness when most people had lost everyone they'd ever loved and cared about. And it was a way to ensure humanity survived. Although Marcus wasn't sure how he'd feel about bringing a kid into this shitty world.

He liked Liberty just fine, but the woman made no bones about the fact that she liked soldiers. Any soldiers. Marcus wanted…something else. Something more.

Cruz snorted. "You've been pretty uptight of late. Getting laid would do us all a favor."

"Can it, Ramos."

Cruz lifted his drink, but the glint in his eyes said he was laughing inside at Marcus' expense. "Then you wouldn't be interested to know a certain pretty, smart and softly sexy brunette is headed our way."

Marcus barely stopped himself from jerking. He flicked his gaze over the crowd and saw Elle wending her way through the throng.

Her dark hair was loose. She usually had it tied up or braided when she was working. She didn't wear any make-up, but her face didn't need it. Clean, fresh and beautiful.

Shit. He lifted his beer and took a huge gulp.

Cruz chuckled. "Still not interested, *amigo*?"

"Fuck you, Cruz."

"I don't think it's me you want to fuck, my friend."

Elle reached them.

"*Hola*, Elle."

"Hi, Cruz." Her gaze landed on Marcus. "Marcus."

He nodded.

"I've just come from the comp lab."

Marcus straightened. "They decoded the map?"

She grimaced. "Sort of. They broke the encryption but they can't decipher the data. There are too many raptor words we don't know."

Marcus swore.

"I'm sorry." She pressed a hand to his forearm. "I'll keep working on it, I promise."

Her touch burned all the way through his skin so that he could swear he felt it in his bones. He pulled away. "We need to locate that comms hub."

She clenched her hands together. "I know."

"Hey, Ellie-girl." Shaw appeared behind her and flicked a finger at her earlobe.

"You're all better?" she asked.

"Sure. The lovely Doc Emerson fixed me right up." He waggled his eyebrows. "I don't mind being injured if I get to stare at a beautiful face while I'm healing." He grabbed her hand. "Next time, you could come visit me and we can play doctor-patient."

Claudia reached over and smacked Shaw in the head. "Quit it, you moron."

Shaw scowled. "You on the other hand, I don't want anywhere near me when I'm healing. You're just as likely to finish me off rather than help me get better."

Claudia's smile was thin. "And don't you forget it."

"Listen up," Marcus said. "Elle says Noah and his geeks can't translate the map."

A round of swearing ensued.

"I'll keep working on it," Elle said. "I'm getting much better with the raptor language."

"We know you will, *querida*." Cruz shoved a beer at her. "Here, have a drink, take a seat next to the boss." With a hand on her shoulder he forced her into a chair beside Marcus. "I'll grab us some chips and what passes for salsa around here." He raised a brow at Marcus. "I'll get a fresh brew."

The others drifted away. Marcus watched Elle take a sip of her beer, while her gaze watched the crowd.

"We still on for tomorrow?" she asked.

"Tomorrow?"

"I usually spar with Cruz in the gym. He said he can't make it and that you'd fill in."

Training? This was the first he'd heard about filling in. Damn, his sneaky friend. But one look at Elle's eyes and Marcus couldn't say no. "Yeah. Sure." Great, just what he needed with his control eroded down to zero. Hand-to-hand combat training with Elle. Her in those tight black leggings she favored when she worked out, rolling around on the mats in the gym. Her skin sweaty and flushed with exertion.

Damn.

Suddenly the music stopped. Marcus glanced up and saw Cruz taking the guitar from the previous musician. Cruz settled on the stool, adjusting the instrument. Then he bent over it and started to play.

The music had an undertone to it that Marcus guessed hailed from Cruz's home country of Mexico. Something that urged everyone to get up and dance. But there was also something else alive in it—something that made you think of hot nights, silk sheets and sweaty bodies.

Marcus took another giant swig of his beer.

Elle's gaze was glued to Cruz. "He's so good. When he's playing, it's like there's no one else in the room."

"Yeah, he's good." Marcus let the strumming wash over him. More dancers had joined in, couples swaying and grinding against each other.

It was all too easy to imagine himself holding Elle against him. Her rounded ass nestled into him, swaying to the intoxicating beat. He could hear her sighs of pleasure, feel her push back against him—

Cruz looked up. He grinned at Marcus, like he knew exactly what he was thinking.

Sudden squeals cut through the beautiful, hypnotic music. Across the room, two guys from Squad Four lifted ladies onto their shoulders. Not far from them, a drunken reveler swung a punch at his equally-drunken mate.

Marcus gripped his beer. He had no right thinking anything about Elle Milton. The last thing Elle needed was his rough hands anywhere near her. Marcus decided he'd head back to his room…and take another cold shower.

Just then Liberty caught his gaze, shot him a huge smile and waggled her fingers. She was persistent, he'd give her that. He lifted his beer in salute but gave the tiniest shake of his head.

As the curvy blonde winked at him, Elle looked up. Her gaze cut to Liberty, then him, and then she shot to her feet. "I'll be…heading off now."

Marcus stood and set his beer down. "Me, too. I have—"

"Other plans." Elle backed away. "I'll see you tomorrow. Good night, Marcus."

He watched her hurry away, bumping into Cruz on her way out.

"What was that all about? You scare her off with your ugly mug?"

"Not sure." Marcus stared at the empty doorway. "I'm hitting my bunk. See you tomorrow."

As he headed for his quarters, Marcus knew a cold shower wouldn't be enough. Instead, he suspected a long night was ahead, with a hard on that wouldn't go away no matter what, staring at the ceiling above his bunk and thinking of big blue eyes and creamy skin.

Chapter Three

Marcus finished his last set of bicep curls and set the weights down on the rack. He glanced at his watch.

Elle was late.

Elle was never late.

Screw this. He was going to find her.

He tried her room first. After banging his fist on the door for a full minute, he frowned. Where the hell was she? A door down the hall opened and a teenage girl teetering on the verge of womanhood leaned against the jamb.

"She isn't there, big guy. Didn't come home last night." The girl grinned. "Figured she got lucky."

"Thanks." Marcus ground his teeth together and stalked off down the hall. Had Elle spent the night in some jackass's bunk? He wanted to slam a fist into the wall. He rounded a corner and nearly plowed into someone headed the other way.

"Hey, Marcus."

"Noah." Marcus tried to keep his scowl to a minimum. "Have you seen Elle?"

Noah nodded. "Yep. She spent the night working on that damn map translation. Left her sleeping facedown on the keyboard."

Marcus' rigid muscles relaxed. "Thanks."

Minutes later, he opened the door to the comp lab and there she was.

Fast asleep.

He let himself watch her for a moment. She was everything he'd never known he liked in a woman. Before the invasion, he'd had sex. Quick, hard and over. He'd never really paid much attention to the woman's personality, or even what she looked like, although he'd tended toward tall, fit women who could handle a man his size. Since the invasion, he'd been too damn busy to worry about women.

Except this one.

Her head was turned to the side, her cheek pressed to the metal desk. Her dark lashes were long against the pale cream of her cheek.

She was a woman meant for silk, and fine dining and sunshine. Not stuck in this shithole.

He reached out, wanting to touch her, but let his hand drop to his side. "Elle?"

Her eyes blinked open, the blue of them unfocused. She blinked again and sat bolt upright. "What time is it?"

"Nine o'clock in the morning."

She pushed her hair back off her face. She had the faint outline of the edge of the keyboard on her cheek. "It can't be." She looked at her watch and groaned. "I'm so sorry, Marcus. I missed our session."

"You've been in here all night?"

"I wanted to see if we'd missed anything on the translation. I don't sleep that well anyway, so I figured I'd work."

He crouched down beside her. "All night is above and beyond, Elle. You need to stay rested. The squad needs you. We get called out, we need you in top form."

Her eyes widened. "God, you're right. I never thought of that. I could have endangered—"

He pressed a finger to her lips. "That's not the point. I don't want to see you run yourself into the ground. No more all-nighters, okay?"

She nodded.

"So, did you find anything?"

She huffed out a breath and twisted her long, dark hair into a knot at the base of her neck. "No. There are just too many letters we don't know." Frustration, raw and sharp in her voice. "I need a Rosetta Stone."

"A what?"

"A Rosetta Stone. It was a stone discovered in Egypt in 1799 by a French solider. It had engravings of Ancient Greek on it, and parallel words in another Egyptian script called Demotic, as well as hieroglyphs. It allowed scholars to finally decipher Ancient Egyptian hieroglyphs. The original stone is probably destroyed now." A flash of sorrow in her eyes. "I know London was decimated in the first wave and it was in the British Museum. But the point is, if I could find something like it, that had our language *and* the raptor language on it, I could use it to decipher more raptor text."

Marcus' jaw tightened. "Or we need a translator."

She snorted. "I'm the best we've got—" her shoulders slumped "—and apparently that's not good enough."

"We have a raptor prisoner in the cells."

Her eyes widened. "But he doesn't speak English."

"No, but the Interrogation team got enough out of him to find out about the map to the comms hub. We might be able to get some more info out of him."

She jumped to her feet. "Then let's go."

Whoa...what? "You aren't coming." He wanted her nowhere near the raptor, even if the alien was chained up.

She lifted her chin. "And how well do you know the raptor language?"

Shit. He recognized a couple of words, at best. The damned dinosaur-like aliens spoke mostly in grunts and roars and wrote in a scrawl that looked like scratches to him. "It isn't safe."

She waved a dismissive hand at him. "He's chained up and locked in a cell. And with you there, I can't get much safer." She snatched up a tablet. "I have everything here. I can show the raptor some of the words I want translated."

"Elle..." Jesus. Marcus didn't want her near the alien, but he also didn't want her to see what had to be done to get the creature to talk. The sad fact was that survival wasn't pretty. "He isn't going to just have a chit chat and offer you what you want. Interrogation...it isn't nice or neat."

Her voice lowered. "I know, Marcus. It's them or us. Tough choices have to be made."

Marcus scraped a hand through his hair. "Shit."

She gripped his arm. "I've been your comms officer for six months. I know this is war and it isn't nice. Now, I'm going down to Interrogation whether you're with me or not."

"Fine." He checked the urge to kick something.

They were silent as they navigated the tunnels and took the spiral ramp down to the lower levels. Blue Mountain Base had started life as a little-used military facility. But after the raptor invasion, it had become a home. Because of its excellent defenses, hidden location, and the fact it had the essentials like a power source, running water and a comp system, it had turned out to be the perfect haven they'd so desperately needed.

It also had a section of reinforced cells in the lower levels.

They reached a heavy metal door guarded by a solider in fatigues.

"Steele," the man said with a nod.

"James. We're here to talk to the prisoner."

James nodded. "Captain Bladon's in there. Talk to her first."

"Will do." Marcus pushed Elle through the door with a hand on the small of her back.

"Staff Sergeant Steele. What have we done to deserve the presence of Hell Squad's leader here in our humble environs?"

Marcus nodded at the tall, redheaded woman blocking their way. Laura Bladon, once a member of the Coalition's Navy Intelligence Unit, was young but she ran the prison area with an iron fist. Behind her, the tunnel was lined with thick, reinforced glass windows that looked into the cells.

"Elle is working to decode the map for the comms hub your raptor prisoner gave us intel on."

"But we can't decipher it all," Elle added. "There are too many raptor words we can't translate."

Bladon's eyes narrowed. "You think he's going to help you? It took my team an entire month to get anything out of him."

"We have to try."

Bladon caught Marcus' gaze. "You sure you want a civvy in there?"

Elle straightened. "I'm Squad Six's comms officer. I'm not a civvy."

Bladon raised a russet brow. "All right. Come on, then."

As they followed the captain down the hall, Marcus cursed the choices he kept being forced to make.

***

Elle dragged in a breath and stepped up to the glass.

Her gaze settled on the raptor chained to a metal chair and her pulse tripped.

He was big. But they were all big. Over six-and-a-half feet, the alien had a humanoid body that was all packed muscle, and covered in thick, gray-mottled, scaly skin. Prominent brow ridges and a heavy, elongated jaw dominated his frightening face and large, hairless head.

Sensing them, he looked up and stared at them. His eyes glowed deep red. Elle could almost see the hatred and a vicious desire to kill within them. She shivered. Then he opened his mouth in something resembling a snarl, baring razor-sharp teeth.

Everything inside her shook. For a second, she was back in that dark closet in her parents' house, listening to her mother's screams.

"Elle?"

Marcus' gravelly rasp drew her back to the present. She wasn't that girl anymore and now she was fighting back. "Open the door."

She heard Marcus mutter under his breath but he pushed the door open.

"I'll be waiting out here if you need anything," Bladon said.

As the door closed behind them, the raptor's hellish gaze zeroed in on them. Elle was grateful for Marcus' solid presence beside her.

Marcus crossed his arms over his chest and glared at the raptor. "You scare her…in *any* way…and I'll make you hurt."

Swallowing, Elle stepped forward, holding the tablet out. "I need to understand these words."

The raptor bared his teeth again and let out a hissing noise.

Up close, she saw blood staining his skin, and ugly wounds that the chains at his wrists and ankles had left. Her stomach turned over. She really didn't want to know what they'd done to get him to talk.

"This word." She pointed at the strange alien scrawl. "I think it means wind. Or air." She fanned the air with her hand.

The raptor lifted his chin, looked over her shoulder at the wall, and stayed silent.

"This word." She pointed to another. "What does it mean?"

The raptor lunged against his chains, rocking the chair, and let out a loud growl. Elle jumped backward.

Suddenly Marcus was there, between her and the alien, slamming the creature and his chair back against the wall. "Do it again. I want to hurt you, you bastard."

Marcus' low words had the right effect, and the raptor dropped his gaze.

Elle steadied herself. She stepped forward once more. "Let's try again."

They kept at it for over an hour. The raptor did know a few English words, but not many. And despite Marcus getting physical with him, he didn't share much.

As they left the cell, Elle's shoulders sagged. "One word. That's all we got."

"It's more than we had." Marcus flexed his hands.

She stared at the blood staining his knuckles. She hated that he'd had to do that.

He noticed her looking and thrust his hands in his pockets.

"*Fly*. It doesn't really help much," she said.

Captain Bladon met them. "If you leave the words with me, I'll have my team continue working with him."

Elle stared at her tablet. "Working with him" was such an innocuous way to say it. She had a choice to make. To leave her notes, and give permission for that…being to be tortured. Butterflies flitted in her belly. Not pretty, gentle ones, but ones with razor-edged wings.

The raptor, for all his invading and killing, was still a living, breathing being. She thought again of her mother's screams, of all the blood soaking into the carpet. Of Marcus and the others going out every day to fight. Elle slowly nodded. "I'll send them through to your comp."

As Elle and Marcus headed back up to the main part of the tunnels, she felt exhaustion dragging on her. "I'll take another look at the map document. See if I can—"

"You need to get some sleep."

She knew he sometimes did back-to-back missions without much rest. He must think she was weak. "All right."

He reached out and tucked a strand of her hair back behind her ear. "Grab a few hours of sleep and then meet me in the gym."

"What?"

"We still have a training session to do."

Her chest tightened. Time with Marcus. Alone. "Okay." She headed down the tunnel to her room, excitement lightening her steps.

"And Elle?"

She glanced over her shoulder. With his broad shoulders and muscled bulk, he seemed to fill the entire tunnel.

"Don't look at that translation again. Get some sleep. I mean it."

Chapter Four

Marcus blocked Elle's kick. She came at him again and he knocked her leg away with his forearm. He was careful not to use his full strength. She was lucky if she weighed sixty kilograms and he was twice that.

"Good," he said. "Again."

She nodded, bouncing on the balls of her feet. Dogged determination was etched on her face. She swiped her arm across her sweaty brow. Dark strands of hair stuck to her damp skin.

Then she attacked.

Roundhouse kick. Step, turn. Side kick. That one packed enough strength to make him grunt. A kick aimed at his head that he deflected. Then she moved in close and slammed a fist into his gut.

He caught her hand before it connected, spun her and yanked her up against him. Her back was pressed to his chest, her rounded ass nestled against his crotch. *Dammit.* He was going to kill Cruz.

"Don't bother trying to punch." God, he loved the feel of her against him. "You have to get too close. Raptors are bigger, stronger. Kick to incapacitate, to buy a bit of time, and then run."

"I suck at this, don't I?" Her voice was quiet.

"No." She was actually getting pretty darn good. "But you aren't physically strong enough to take on a raptor at close quarters, no matter your training or your armor. Not many of us are. Got it?"

She nodded. Her hair tickled his face and her scent filled his senses—something with flowers and coconut that was all Elle, mixed with healthy feminine sweat. His cock twitched and he recited a few mental curses.

He set her away and dragged in some air. "Again."

She lifted her chin and rushed at him, her kick aimed for his midsection. He blocked and watched her move. Her kicks would never be powerful enough to do much damage, but damn, she moved gracefully. Like a dancer.

"Come on, Elle. Quit playing around."

"Playing around?" Her jaw set, something flashing in her eyes. Yeah, he'd noted that determination in her before. First, when she'd lobbied to become Hell Squad's comms officer. He'd fought just as hard not to have her.

But she'd found ways to prove to him she was the best person for the job. Getting extra intel for their missions. Filling in when their old comms officer was sick. Quietly winning over his squad until he'd had no choice.

Yeah, he saw her determination every time he was planning a mission or out in the field. Elle bent over backwards to do the best job she could for Hell Squad. He wondered what ghosts drove her burning need to prove herself.

Marcus remembered the night he'd found her. It was a few weeks after the alien invasion. The base had been a chaos of military personnel all jostling for command. But Marcus and his team had kept going out and bringing in survivors. Elle had been with a rag-tag group who'd made it out of the city. She'd been covered in raptor blood and shell-shocked, but she'd still been helping to comfort other survivors.

His brief foray down memory lane cost him. A sudden, hard kick to his knee took him down. Her slight weight slammed into him and he was enough off balance to hit the mats hard. Elle landed on top of him, straddling his chest.

"Yes!" She grinned and pumped a fist in the air. "How's that for playing, Steele?"

Hell, she was so goddamned beautiful. He stared at her face and realized he rarely saw that free, easy smile on her. He wished he could see it all the time.

"She got you, Steele," a voice called out.

Marcus managed to rip his gaze from Elle. Roth Masters, leader of Squad Nine was doing bicep curls with a couple of members of his team at the free weights in the far corner of the gym.

"Yeah. She did." Marcus looked back at Elle and their gazes met. Caught.

Her smile melted away and Marcus felt the air leave his lungs. The air around them turned charged.

She licked her lips. "Marcus—"

"Nice work, Elle." Roth appeared above them. "Felling an oaf like Steele takes some skill."

Elle scrambled off him and onto her feet. "I think I surprised him."

A tiny smile tweaked Roth's lips. "Yeah, I reckon you've been doing that from the first day he met you."

Marcus shot Masters a scowl, and without bothering to use his hands, leaped to his feet. "Don't you have a mission to plan or training to conduct?"

"Nope. Watching you get your butt kicked by a girl is much more satisfying."

"Screw you, Masters." But Marcus knew the ribbing was all in good fun.

Roth smiled, but then his rugged face turned serious. "I heard you recovered the raptor comms map but the geek squad can't get a location from it."

"You heard right." The burn of frustration was bitter.

"There are too many unknown raptor words," Elle added.

"And our guest downstairs wasn't any help?" Roth asked.

Marcus shook his head. "Doesn't know enough English to be much good to us. Elle tells me she needs a Rosetta Stone."

"The stone used to decipher Egyptian hieroglyphs?"

Marcus raised his brows. "How's a grunt like you know that?"

"I'm not stupid." Then a frown covered Roth's face. "You know, I might have seen something like that on our last mission." He spun. "Hey, Mac, remember that raptor research center we raided two days ago?"

Mac was short for Mackenna. The short, petite woman wandered over. Marcus knew more than one man had underestimated the female soldier who had a black belt in something deadly and took no prisoners. "Yeah, boss. They'd taken over a library in the city. Had a load of that damned organic cabling of theirs all over the place."

"Do you remember much about the raptor comp screens we saw?"

"A bit. They had a bunch of raptor gibberish on them but there was English as well. Looked like they'd hacked into the library's network. Also saw a bunch of those black crystals they use to store their data."

Marcus had seen the black crystals before and knew that Noah had had some success pulling data off them.

"What were they doing there?" Elle asked.

"Not sure, exactly." Roth shrugged his broad shoulders. "My best guess, they were trying to decode our data. We went in to investigate, but it turned into a rescue mission. They had a few librarians they'd taken prisoner."

"Prisoner?" Marcus frowned. "Never seen them keep prisoners long."

Roth shrugged. "Librarians didn't know why the raptors kept them. They had been locked up in the dark and were lucky to get a little bit of food and water."

Marcus didn't know why the raptors wanted human prisoners, but whatever the reason, it couldn't be good.

Elle turned to Marcus. "We need to convince General Holmes to send a team in to recover these crystals. They might just give us enough data to help us translate the comms map."

"Yeah—" An alarm blared through the gym. "Fuck." The squads were needed for something urgent.

"Got to go." Roth waved and jogged out of the gym, followed by his team members.

"Go," Elle urged Marcus. "I'll get to the Comms Control Room and if I get a chance, I'll talk to the general about recovering the crystals."

Marcus nodded, his mind already turning to prepping the team. "You tell him Hell Squad wants to go in and get the crystals."

"Will do."

He started to turn.

"Marcus?"

He paused and glanced at her.

Her blue eyes were direct. "Be careful out there."

"Always." For the first time he wished he had a bit of Cruz's good looks or Shaw's charm. "I'm too tough to die."

***

The Hawk swept in low over the trees, heading

back to base. The occupants were mostly silent.

Marcus touched the button on the side of his combat helmet and the thin, high-tech thermoplastic retracted back into his armor. His shoulder throbbed. A fucking raptor had gotten close enough to take a swipe at him and the damn aliens had bloody sharp claws. It had managed to yank off part of his armor and leave a gouge that was still stinging and bleeding sluggishly.

He glanced at his team. Cruz sat silently, with his head in his hands. Gabe and Zeke were pacing—as best they could in the confined space—with their carbines clenched tightly in their hands, and Claudia was cleaning her weapon with a maniacal intensity. Even Shaw was quiet. He sat with his head against the wall, staring out the window.

They'd been sent out to rescue a group of survivors headed for the base.

The raptors had found them first.

Hell Squad had fought and chased the bastards off, but many of the survivors hadn't made it. He scraped a hand down his face. After months of scavenging and hiding, those people had died just kilometers from safety, cut down like animals in the dirt.

But he knew what hurt his team most was the little girl they hadn't been able to save.

She'd had her hair pulled up in two tails off the sides of her head. Someone had cared enough to scrounge some grungy purple ribbons for her. She'd almost reached the second Hawk when a raptor had shot her in the back with one of their poison weapons.

Fuck. Marcus looked outside again. He knew he'd see that little girl's face when he went to sleep that night. He stared, unseeing, down at the trees lining the Blue Mountains. There was speculation that the thick trees were one of the things helping to keep the base safe. Raptors didn't appear to like being amongst the trees, and as a result, they stuck to the city, open farmland and even the desert.

Oh, the bastards had to know they were here somewhere. But combined with the heavy forest, the entrances to the base were thankfully well hidden—and Holmes had entire teams dedicated to keeping it that way.

They passed over a river and a wide expanse of rocks. Suddenly, the rocks began moving. The giant doors above the Hawk hangars—disguised to blend into the scenery—retracted. The Hawk's rotors tilted and they began their descent.

Marcus shifted his carbine and his injury burned. Shit. He hoped it wasn't bad enough to require a trip to the infirmary. He hated the infirmary.

The Hawk touched down.

He slid the doors back. "Everyone get some rest. Grab a beer, watch a movie, find someone to fuck. Work out the bad and get your head screwed back on straight. We should have a mission soon to recover some crystals that'll help decode the map we found."

He got nods and grunts in reply.

"And you, *amigo*?" Cruz murmured. "What will you do to rest?"

"I'm fine." He couldn't rest. He had drone footage he wanted to review and he needed to do some prelim planning for the next mission.

One of Cruz's dark brows rose. "This must remind you of—"

"Don't want to talk about it, Ramos." Cruz was a damned good friend, but that also meant he knew exactly what buttons to push. Instead, Marcus pushed back. "Why don't we talk about you? The fact you're getting quieter, playing the guitar less, fucking less? What's going on?"

Cruz's mouth snapped shut. With a final look at Marcus, he turned and leaped out of the Hawk.

As the others left the Hawk, Marcus stared at Cruz's back. Damn, he was worried. Cruz was normally all charming smiles and laughs that women said were sexy. He wasn't usually wound so tight he might explode.

With a sigh, Marcus jumped down from the Hawk, and his shoulder throbbed again.

Then he saw Holmes and Elle waiting for him. Dealing with Cruz was going to have to wait. He headed over to meet them.

"Well done bringing the survivors in," Holmes said. "They're already being checked over by Medical and are being assigned quarters."

Marcus' jaw worked. "We left most of them lying dead in the dirt."

"You can't save everyone."

The little girl's terrified face flashed through his

head. He managed a nod.

"And I need you and the team ready to head out again."

He stopped. Saw the other members of his team moving ahead of him stop and turn back. "What?"

Elle stepped forward. "The general's authorized the mission to recover the crystals."

"We need to find that comms hub, Steele. Whatever it takes."

Looked like they were going to wade through more raptor muck much sooner than he'd thought. "Okay. But we need a few hours. We have minor injuries and the guys need some downtime."

Holmes looked like he wanted to argue, which made Marcus want to punch the guy's perfect face.

"Fine."

Elle cleared her throat. "There's a catch."

Marcus' jaw tightened. There was always something. "I'm listening."

She shoved her hands in her pockets. "I talked more with Roth and his team. They saw loads of crystals."

Marcus frowned. "So we'll grab all of them."

"Hundreds. You can't grab all of them. You need to find the right ones."

"You're saying we'll need to look at what's on them?"

She nodded.

"I can do it."

She shook her head. "You don't know enough raptor."

"So, teach me what to look for."

"You know that won't work. I've been studying this for over six months. You can't just have a ten-minute lesson."

Holmes nodded. "She's right. You won't have time to decipher on the run. You need someone with the skills to do it quickly." The general glanced at Elle. "Elle will be coming with you."

Marcus' heart stopped. "No—"

The general's jaw tightened. "She's the best we have. She's going."

Dammit. Marcus' hands curled into fists. "No. Absolutely not. I don't want her."

Chapter Five

Elle felt her heart slam against her ribs. *Marcus didn't want her.*

Struggling not to let her feelings show on her face, she set her shoulders back. Marcus didn't think she could do it. It reminded her that he hadn't wanted her for their comms officer either. Dammit, hadn't she proven herself by now?

General Holmes' voice turned hard. "Steele, we have to do what's best for the mission—"

"Sending an untrained and unprepared civilian into a warzone is not what's best for the mission." With a vicious glance at her, Marcus stormed out of the room.

A part of Elle wanted to shrink into a little ball. She looked up and saw Claudia, wearing her scuffed body armor, her dark hair pulled back in one long braid, looking at Elle, a faint smile on her face.

The other part of Elle was pissed.

That taunting smirk made Elle's quivering belly harden. *No way*. This mission was too important. She wanted to help. She wouldn't sit idly by and just be another bystander waiting to be rescued. That's why she'd volunteered in the comms department in the first place. She wanted to help. She *needed* to help.

Pivoting, she strode after Marcus.

His long legs had eaten up the ground between them and she had to jog to catch him. He was ripping pieces of his body armor off.

For a second, her gaze snagged on his big, muscular biceps.

Elle steeled herself. "Marcus!"

He kept going.

He was going to listen to her, dammit. She snagged the sleeve of his shirt. "I can do this."

He came to a halt so fast she almost ran into him.

"You have no fucking idea what it's like out there." He spun. His tough face was set in rigid lines. It would have sent a lesser person running.

"Do you know what it's like to have raptors raining down on you? To be covered in gore?" He tugged at his shirt, it was soaked dark red.

Under his hard green gaze her confidence wavered, but she stiffened her spine. "I have an idea. I survived the attack. I watch it on my screen, I hear the laser fire, the roars of the aliens. I've heard people die. I feel the worry, the anxiety knowing you…the team…are out there. I know what it's like."

He shook his head. "Hearing it is nothing like experiencing it."

Sometimes she thought it was worse. Hearing him firing his weapon, yelling orders at his squad as raptors charged them, while she was stuck, unable to help, in the base. Now she had a chance to do something.

She took a step forward until her boots hit his. "I am not some stupid, little civvy with nothing to offer. I know the realities. I know if we don't pull this mission off, we'll be stuck in this place like rats forever. Waiting in our hole until the raptors sniff us out and finish us humans off for good. Until they help themselves to our planet and its resources and leave it a desolate ruin." She sucked in a breath, her chest heaving. "I can *do* this."

His jaw hardened. "I know you can. That's not the damn problem." He turned and stomped down the hall.

Elle blinked, her brow scrunching in confusion. What was the issue then? "What, Marcus? You *need* to take me on this mission. What the hell is your problem?"

He moved so fast it was shocking. He pushed her up against the smooth tunnel wall, his big body crowding her in.

He smelled hot, sweaty and bloody, and heat poured off his muscular frame. God, he made her feel so…small. She felt a lick of something molten inside.

Marcus leaned in until his face was an inch from hers. "My problem is you."

Pain lanced through her. Okay, he couldn't make it any clearer that he thought she wasn't right for the job. She quivered against him. "I know you never wanted me as comms officer for Six. I know you thought I couldn't do it, but haven't I proven that I can?"

His head lowered, his intense gaze roaming her face until it stopped. Was he looking at her lips? A flicker of heat in her belly. No, Marcus would never feel that way about her, despite her most secret fantasies.

"You've done a great job, but I don't want you in the field."

His deep voice shivered through her. Everything about this tough, battle-hardened man drew her in. His voice, his strength, his resolve. She wanted to lean into his strength, let him take all the worry and burden off her for a few precious seconds.

But he already shouldered too much. He was already the one all of mankind depended on to go out there every day and risk his life to protect them.

"I need to do this, Marcus." She stared straight into his eyes. That bright, vivid green she sometimes saw in her dreams. "I *need* to help."

He groaned, his head dropping forward until his hot lips brushed her ear. "Ellianna."

No one called her that anymore. She'd left Ellianna, the society girl, behind the day the aliens had destroyed her world. But she guessed that was all Marcus saw when he looked at her.

Her voice dropped to a whisper and she forced the next words out, even though it felt like they were ripped from her soul. "I need to matter."

She'd never really mattered to anyone—not her mother, not to the man she thought she'd marry, and least of all, the father who'd barely noticed she was there.

Marcus was silent, his entire body vibrating with tension. His breath was hot on the side of her neck and she felt all the muscles in her body turn to jelly. "Do you want me to beg? Please, Marcus—"

"No, I don't want you to beg."

His lips brushed her earlobe and she closed her eyes. God, did he know he was killing her with that accidental contact? She wanted to give into the gnawing inside her and grab him. Hold him tight, explore those hard muscles, taste him…

"I know you can do this, Elle. I just want to keep you safe."

She pulled in a breath. He was always protecting everybody else, never giving any consideration to his own life.

Again, his lips brushed her skin, this time the side of her neck. She shivered and barely managed to swallow a groan.

"And you do matter," he said. "To me."

***

Back off, Steele. His brain was telling him one thing, but with Elle's slim, enticing frame pressed against him, his body wanted something else. Shit, it was lucky he hadn't taken off his lower-body armor, or she'd feel his hard cock digging into her belly.

He fought for some control. In the field, control was so damned easy. He commanded his squad, covered all the bases, planned every step but was always ready to flex when the shit hit, as it always did.

But with this woman, he always felt like he never had a handle on anything. He shouldn't even have his dirty, death-covered hands anywhere near her creamy skin.

But with everything churning inside him and being this close to her… Marcus lost the battle he'd been fighting for months.

He pressed his lips to the silky skin of her jaw, then moved up and claimed her mouth.

Her full lips parted on a gasp. And he took full advantage.

He wasn't gentle, had never been gentle, he plundered. He slid his tongue in her mouth and her taste hit him like a rush. Sweet, so fucking sweet.

Her hands slid up into his hair. She moved against him, making little noises in the back of her throat.

And she kissed him back.

She kissed the hell out of him.

Lost in her, in that special taste that was Elle, he held on, taking everything he could and loving that she gave as good as she got.

But slowly, reality filtered in. He had her pinned against the wall. Mauling her. Worse, he was dirty and grimy and covered in blood—some of it his own.

Dredging up some strength from God-only-knew where, Marcus pulled himself away from her. Both of their chests were heaving.

Jesus, those big blue eyes hit him hard. If she ever found out that all she had to do was look at him and he wouldn't be able to deny her a single thing, he'd be in a whole lot of trouble. *Focus, Steele. On the mission. Not her.*

"Okay, you're in." Dammit, he wanted to ram a fist into the wall. "But you'll do exactly as I say, wear armor at all times, and you won't leave my side. No matter what. Got it?"

She blinked, taking a second to process. Then her eyes lit up. "I'll do everything you tell me."

God, her earnest words stabbed at him. Made him imagine her doing things that had nothing to do with the mission.

"I'm going to clean up, grab some food. Two hours and we're heading back out there to kick some raptor butt. Go and find some body armor that won't swamp you and I'll meet you back at the Hawk."

She nodded, her eyes alive. With excitement, fear…he wasn't sure.

"Marcus, about—"

He heard the questioning tone in her voice but he didn't want to talk about that kiss. At least, not now. He cut her off. "Find yourself a weapon. You'll need something if you have to take a raptor down at close quarters."

She swallowed hard. "You think that'll happen?"

"Anything can happen out there." The thought of her tangling with one of those damned alien beasts made his gut churn. He'd protect her, no matter what he had to do. "Two hours. Landing pads."

She nodded. "Okay. But Marcus?"

"Yeah."

"After the mission, we will talk about that kiss." She turned and hurried down the tunnel.

Marcus forced himself to head to his quarters. All he really wanted to do was drag her away and lock her up to keep her safe.

And dammit, he also wanted to do a hell of a lot more.

When he reached his quarters, he tore off the rest of his armor, then his clothes, and stepped into a cold shower. He welcomed the sting of the freezing water. It hit the gash on his shoulder and washed the blood away. He glanced at the wound. He'd been right—it wasn't as bad as he'd first thought. A bit of med-gel and it should be good. He'd have another scar to add to the collection.

He dropped his forehead to the faded tile. Damn, he wasn't looking forward to this mission. Big blue eyes swam into his vision. That dark hair he wanted to wrap around his hand. He could picture her spread out on his bunk, all slim limbs and smooth skin.

Jesus. He slid a soapy hand down his stomach, circled his cock. He had to find some damned control because he was going to need all his focus to take Elle into the heart of hell and then get her out alive.

***

Marcus slammed his armor into place and yanked

the fastening tight. Around him in the squad locker room, some of his team were doing the same.

Thirty minutes to go time.

"Where are Frost and Shaw?" Marcus barked.

Cruz checked his carbine. "They'll be here. I think Claudia was helping Elle find some armor."

Marcus paused. The idea of tough-as-nails Claudia helping Elle…that just didn't seem right. "And Shaw?"

Zeke leaned forward and waggled his eyebrows. "Think he got nabbed by that cute little redhead who works down in supplies."

Cruz closed his locker. "You sure you want to take her on this mission?"

Marcus knew his second wasn't talking about Claudia or the redhead. "Don't have a choice."

"There's always a choice, my friend."

With extra force, Marcus slammed his locker closed. "You don't think if there was another way, I'd take it?" The men fell silent and he felt them watching him. The anger pounding through him was like a raging river. He shoved his combat knife into the sheath on his thigh. "You think I want her anywhere near the raptors?"

"No, but—"

"I don't want her hurt. I'd gut myself first."

Gabe and Zeke stopped their final preparations to listen.

Marcus released a harsh breath. "We need those crystals to find the alien comms hub, and…for some insane reason, she wants this. I don't know, she has some need to prove herself. All I can do is try and keep her safe."

"We'll all keep her safe," Gabe said, his gray eyes intense.

Marcus knew the quiet man was giving him a promise. As he looked at the others, they nodded as well. The tightness inside his chest eased…a little.

He turned to Cruz. "If the mission goes to hell, if I go down, your priority is to get Elle out."

His friend nodded. "You got it, Marcus."

The locker room door opened, and Claudia strode in. Her dark hair was braided, and she wore a tank top that showed off muscled arms. "Hey, Marcus, we might turn your princess into a warrior, yet."

As Claudia opened her locker and started pulling out her armor, Marcus forced his breathing to slow, in an attempt to stay calm. "She's ready?"

"Yeah." Claudia pressed her chest armor into place. "She's nervous as hell, but she's hiding it. She might look like she belongs at a dinner party, but nobody can fault her for courage."

The door opened again, and this time Shaw sauntered in. His tawny hair was mussed and he had a satisfied look on his face. "Ladies."

Zeke snorted. "Only you would squeeze in a quickie before heading into hell."

The sniper shrugged and grinned. "Any time is a good time for a quickie, Jackson."

Claudia shot him a scathing look and turned back to her locker. "Some women prefer a man who can last more than a few minutes."

Shaw stiffened. "I can—"

"Don't start, you two," Marcus warned. "We're meeting Elle at the Hawk in fifteen minutes, so hustle."

Shaw frowned. "Elle? What do you mean? Don't tell me she's coming with us?"

"Didn't you read the mission brief?" Claudia asked snidely.

He ignored her, his gaze on Marcus. "Are you crazy? We can't take her into the heart of raptor territory. It's no place for a woman—" he glanced at Claudia, who was already rounding on him "—without combat training."

Zeke snorted again. "Good save."

Marcus slashed a hand through the air. "I don't want to take Elle, either. But we need her skills. We'll all have to keep her safe, get the mission done and then get the hell out of there. Got it?"

Everyone nodded. Marcus knew if there was anyone he could trust, it was his team.

Hell Squad would help him keep Elle safe, no matter what.

He swung his carbine over his shoulder. "All right, let's move out."

Chapter Six

The quadcopter's engines were silent but the wind rushing past the open sides was a constant roar in Elle's ears.

She gripped the bar attached to the roof and tried to keep her balance. She half-expected a raptor ship to appear beside them. Shaped like giant flying dinosaurs, they'd been nicknamed pteros after pterosaurs or pterodactyls.

But the Hawk's pilot would have the copter's illusion system running. It didn't completely cloak the Hawk from view but it messed with its signature on raptor scans, blurred them a bit on visual, and used directed sound waves to distort any noise and make the enemy think the copter was somewhere other than its present location.

It didn't make her feel much better. Fear was like a slow-eating acid in her veins. She could only hope no one noticed how badly her hands were shaking.

The rest of Hell Squad lounged around her. She wouldn't say they were relaxed, just focused. Shaw gripped the edge of the door, staring out toward the horizon, his long-range laser rifle clutched securely in his other hand. Claudia sat at the back, checking her carbine. For the third time.

Cruz sat quietly, staring at the floor, his lean, handsome face composed, while Gabe and Zeke murmured to each other in the back. And Marcus was leaning into the cockpit, talking with the pilot about their landing zone.

Elle fiddled with the edge of her armor. She looked the part, even if the armor was a little big on her, and her tiny, high-tech earpiece felt foreign. And the armor took a little getting used to. Because of the exoskeleton built into it, it helped her move faster and jump higher. Still, she felt like a little girl playing dress-up.

They had to get those data crystals. Everyone was depending on her to get them there.

She lifted her arm. The shiny, portable comp screen was strapped securely to her wrist. It showed the location of the library where Roth and his squad had seen the crystals. She'd be doing some of her usual job on the mission, but the rest of it was in Noah's hands. He'd volunteered to be their temporary comms officer for this trip.

She swallowed, trying to clear the giant lump in her throat. She'd faced down Marcus to come on this mission, and now her nerves were eating at her like hundreds of tiny ants.

Looking for a distraction, she glanced out the side of the Hawk at the ground below.

Destruction. As far as the eye could see.

Sydney had been the shining capital of the United Coalition—the combination of several Commonwealth countries including Australia,

Canada, India, the United Kingdom, and the United States of America. Since advanced supersonic travel had made the distance between the member countries negligible, they'd chosen the beautiful Australian harbor city as their new capital.

It had been a center of commerce, arts and culture. Once upon a time, the city center had been filled with huge, towering spires that housed all the global companies headquartered there.

Now all she saw on the horizon were a few shattered shards still reaching into the sky, like bony fingers, pleading for salvation.

Directly below the quadcopter, bathed in the afternoon sun, was what had once been the suburbs. At one time, alive with families and life. The whole area was now just rubble. The raptor hunting parties had cleared out any stranded survivors a long time ago. Arching her neck, Elle thought she saw the area that had been her parents' estate, just north of the city. Her home.

It was so surreal to see the extent of the devastation. It left her feeling hollow.

She'd hidden for several weeks after the first waves of alien attacks. But eventually, she'd found the courage to flee the city—that remained under siege—with a small group of stragglers. They'd found some cars and a small amount of fuel, escaped an attack by the raptors, and were finally picked up by Hell Squad at the foothills of the Blue Mountains.

She still remembered Marcus surveying their

small group. He'd been so…intimidating. She'd wondered at the time if he ever smiled. Her lips quirked at the memory. He did smile. Not often, but when he did it was worth the wait. She glanced at him now and saw he was no longer talking with the pilot. Instead, he was watching her with an intensity that made her feel like she was naked.

She glanced away, and looked again at the view below, but now all she could think about was that kiss.

Hot, possessive and so, so good.

The kiss of a man who wanted a woman.

But he was acting professional, so she would, too. For now.

Find the crystals, decode the map, destroy the raptor comms hub. That's all she could allow herself to think about right now. She knew that many people back at base thought that if they managed to destroy the raptors or drive them away, life would go back to the way it had been before.

With the destroyed city staring back at her, she knew things would never be the same, ever again. Her shoulders sagged under the empty feeling of chances lost, of what had been.

But at the same time, Elle realized that she didn't want to go back to the person she'd been before. She didn't want to be the shallow, self-absorbed Ellianna Milton who'd never finished her university degree, who'd partied all night, and still lived with her parents because it was convenient, and free.

Her gaze zeroed back to Marcus. His dark head was bent now and so she looked her fill. She'd changed. Over the past year, she'd seen people with values that mattered. People who risked their lives for others, no questions asked. And who did it over and over again. The kind of person she wanted to be.

She fiddled idly with her armor for a minute before she realized a fastening wasn't quite done up and it gaped under her right arm. She jiggled it, trying to get it sorted, without success. She huffed out a breath. Some soldier she was, she couldn't even dress herself.

She lifted her head and saw Claudia smirking at her. Dammit, the other woman might be a trained soldier, but that grating grin made Elle want to smack her.

"Let me."

Marcus stepped in front of Elle. His hands brushed hers away and he snapped the fastening closed, his fingers brushing her side for a second. She sucked in quick breath.

He ran his hands over the molded carbon fiber pieces, checking them. "A little big but not bad."

"Claudia found it for me. Not sure why, I don't think she likes me," Elle muttered.

"She doesn't like anyone." Amusement underscored his tone. "But actually I think she likes you just fine. She told me you're the best comms officer she's ever had."

"Really?" Elle was floored. "But she's always laughing at me. Not out loud, just these little smirks—"

A snort from behind Marcus. *Oh God, she'd heard.*

"Princess, that's for Marcus' benefit, not yours." Claudia stepped into view, her carbine slung over her shoulder. "I just love seeing him squirm."

Elle frowned. "I don't understand."

"Shut it, Frost." Marcus turned his back on Claudia, blocking Elle's view of the other woman. "Did you find a weapon?"

Elle slipped a hand into the side holster on the armor and withdrew a small thermo pistol.

He took it, checked it, handed it back to her. "It'll do. It isn't too heavy for you and it's easy to use. Just point and shoot. You have extra ammunition?"

She put the pistol away and nodded. She had a stash of thermo bullets. When fired, a chemical reaction was triggered in the bullets that made them heat up to scorching temperatures. Hot enough to penetrate tough, scaled skin.

"I'm nervous." The words slipped out of her.

He set one finger under her chin and tilted it up. His green gaze was steady. "Nerves are good. You go in cocky, you get yourself killed."

"Okay."

He looked at his heavy-duty watch. "Five minutes until we land. Ready?"

No. A part of her wanted to curl up and stay in relative safety on the Hawk. She straightened her shoulders. She wasn't that girl anymore. Besides, Marcus would be by her side.

"I'm ready."

He turned to the team. "Hell Squad, ready to go to hell?"

"Hell, yeah!" Elle raised her voice to mix with the rest of the team. "The devil needs an ass-kicking."

***

Marcus activated his combat helmet and once it was in place, leaped the couple of meters from the hovering quadcopter to the cracked concrete. He kept his gaze up, searching for any waiting raptors.

Around him, his team also hit the ground. They crouched low, guns up, and headed for cover.

Marcus turned and held his arms out for Elle. She didn't hesitate to jump. He caught her slight weight, took an extra second to hold her close, then set her on her feet. "Let's go."

They jogged toward what had once been a shopping mall. Now the large sign above the doors hung lopsided, and all the windows in the triple-story building were broken. In the parking lot, cars were piled on top of each other and tipped over, as though they were nothing more than toys that an angry child had kicked.

Or an angry rex.

"It's so quiet," Elle whispered.

Yeah. Too quiet.

They were ten meters from the safety of the mall

entrance when raptor fire ripped across the ground in front of them. Elle skidded to a halt, throwing her arms up.

Marcus didn't stop to think. He tackled her to the ground and rolled them into cover behind a car.

They stopped with him on top of her, both of them breathing heavily. He gripped her face in his gloved fingers. "Elle, you okay?" God, she hadn't been hit, had she? Standard raptor weapons shot high-velocity poison that burned and paralyzed, while their snipers shot razor-sharp projectiles made of a bone-like substance. Either was deadly. He felt the racing drum of her pulse in her temple.

"I'm okay." Her words were breathless as her hands clamped over his wrists.

Shit. He was twice her size and squishing her. He rolled off her and crouched. "Stay down." He lifted his carbine and sighted a raptor sniper on the roof. He heard his team returning fire and through the scope, the reptilian humanoid came into view. For a second, Marcus wondered if the scientists' theories were right. That this alien was what the Earth's dinosaurs might have evolved into over millions of years if they'd survived.

He gave his head a tiny shake and blocked everything out. It was second nature. "Get the job done" had always been his motto, one he'd learned from his Marine father. Marcus sighted the head of the ugly raptor, right between his red eyes. *One, two, three.* Marcus pulled the trigger.

There was a spray of blood and the raptor fell backward out of view.

"Let's go." He yanked Elle up and pulled her toward the others.

"A little welcoming committee," Cruz said.

"Yeah." Marcus nodded at his second. "They know we're here." He glanced at Elle. "Time to do your stuff. Where to?"

She studied her little screen, her brow furrowed. "Through the mall. The library's situated on the street on the other side."

"Let's move." Marcus motioned them on.

"Wait." Elle reached up and pressed her fingers to his face. Her touch was electric, he froze.

"You got nicked by something." Her finger ran over his stubbled cheek.

He clamped a hand over her wrist, held her touch to his cheek for the briefest second before he pulled it away. "I'm fine."

She nodded and stepped back. Over her head, Marcus saw his team all grinning at him like idiots.

"Into position." He growled the command, but inside he felt a little glow of something he couldn't focus on right now. He studied Elle's dark head. He had to keep her safe.

His team moved into their positions. They were a motley crew but Hell Squad got the job done. The rules had changed since the invasion. Now a little rebel thinking was needed because that was what they'd become in their own world.

Elle kept pace beside him. As they moved through the mall, past shops with their windows still displaying their wares, she mimicked the others on the team, staying in cover. Moving fast. He knew she had to be afraid, but she was steady. *Good girl, hang in there.* A quick learner, his Elle.

Not yours, Steele. They moved through the old food court. All the chairs were empty, but the tables were still covered in old trays and fast-food wrappers. Like people had only just left moments before.

Where the hell were the raptors? Marcus clutched his carbine tighter. He almost wished for an attack. It would make him less nervous.

They made it to the other end of the mall, but Marcus' neck was tingling. This was far too easy. They were deep in raptor territory, close to one of their key installations. No way they'd let them just waltz in.

"Razor sharp, Hell Squad," he murmured. "They're here somewhere."

They stepped out onto the street. It was deserted except for twisted steel, rusting cars and rubble.

Marcus warily led the team out, Elle close at his side, moving into the open. He'd be happy when they were back in cover.

Suddenly, Shaw yelled, "Canids!"

Fuck. Marcus saw the pack of fast-moving creatures racing toward them.

Canids were the equivalent to raptor hunting dogs. The damned things had a row of sharp spikes along their backs and a mouth of teeth that made razors look dull.

And they loved gnawing on humans.

Chapter Seven

Hell Squad opened fire.

The canids loped in their direction, easily leaping over obstacles, their burning-red eyes fixed on them. Marcus fired with one hand and grabbed Elle with the other, pushing her down.

The front line of creatures fell, letting out wild, inhuman screams as they writhed in pools of their own blood.

"We need to go there!" Elle pointed to a long, low-set building. "That's the library."

"Go!" Marcus pulled her up. She ran, her arms pumping. His team closed in around them, still firing at the next wave of canids.

Marcus hit the door with one shoulder. The metal groaned. He reared back and hit again. It gave way.

Immediately inside sat the library reception desk. Dust coated all the surfaces and trash and dried leaves littered the floor.

Marcus nodded toward the main part of the library. "Keep it quiet," he murmured. "Roth said there were raptors working in here. They might still be around." He looked at Gabe and Zeke. "Bar the door."

One step ahead of Marcus, the brothers had already started the task before Marcus had finished speaking. They'd barely gotten some metal pipes through the door handles when the canids hit it. The door vibrated under the weight of them, and they shrieked. The canids' howls were enough to send shivers through anyone. Gabe and Zeke kept working to strengthen the doors.

"All right, let's find these crystals." Marcus touched his ear. "Noah, we've reached the library."

A hiss of static came across the line. Then Noah's faint voice. "Marcus…raptors jamming…working to…hold tight."

Dammit. Marcus bit off a curse. It didn't change anything, it just left them blind until Noah could get the comms back up. The team fell into position. Cruz took point, followed by Claudia. Marcus kept Elle in the center and Shaw brought up the rear, holding his sniper rifle like it was precious gold.

They passed into the main part of the library and as the doors closed behind them, all the noise cut off. The library had been soundproofed, no doubt to keep the noise of the city out. It was mostly high-tech comp screens and consoles, now silent and covered in dust. But toward the back, the library still had a historic section of paper books lined up on rows of shelves.

A loud humming sound filled the room. Like the whirr of a large machine.

Marcus used hand signals to direct his team. They moved with stealth, constantly scanning ahead for any movement or noise. Moments later,

Gabe and Zeke silently rejoined the group.

Elle stayed close, moving slowly and working hard to be quiet.

They rounded an overturned table. Elle stepped onto glass from one smashed comp screen. It made a faint crunching noise.

A sudden, deep grunt made them all freeze.

Marcus held his closed fist up. Then he inched forward and glanced around a bookshelf.

Three large screens sat on a long desk. He guessed they were what passed for raptor comp screens. They were all liquid black with jagged edges, and had strange golden symbols flashing in the center of them.

Surrounding them, heavy, scale-covered cables tapped into the side of the screens. The cables looked organic and pulsed gently. They were attached to a large black box that was making the humming sound and glowed red intermittently. The geek squad at base had studied some raptor tech the squads had brought home. Most of the alien technology had organic material spliced into it.

Off to the side on a separate table sat an untidy stack of black crystals in the shape of small cubes. More were sitting in a box below.

A raptor sat in front of the screens, perusing the data.

Marcus scanned around. The alien appeared to be alone. He was smaller than the standard warrior raptors.

Gabe inched forward and caught Marcus' gaze.

He held up his large gladius combat knife. The knife all the squad members carried.

Marcus nodded. Gabe was a spooky-good soldier. When Marcus had accepted the man onto Squad Six, he'd heard the rumors. That Gabe had come from some secret military super-soldier program. Marcus had certainly seen the man do some things that didn't seem humanly possible.

The unknown and unexplainable tended to scare people, but Marcus didn't care because Gabe was damned good at his job. Marcus figured everything that had come before the invasion could stay there. None of them were the same people they'd been before.

Elle glanced from Gabe, to the knife, and then to the raptor.

Yeah, the realities of this ugly war of survival were what he'd wanted to protect her from. He gripped her chin and forced her to look at him. Her blue eyes were wide, but steady.

Gabe didn't make a single noise, nor did the raptor as he died.

Marcus waited until Gabe had dragged the body away before he urged Elle forward.

She hurried to the comp screens, grabbed the chair, then paused. Blood stained the edge of the seat. She stared at it for a second before she stiffened her spine and sat. As she studied the raptor symbols on the screen, her brow scrunched. Then she tapped some of them. Data filled the far right screen. Most if it was in English.

"Looks like they're copying ebooks and any other

relevant data from the library's databases." She tapped again, scanning the screens. "They're focusing on anything referencing resources, power generation, computer technology and medical science." She shook her head. "No raptor language on this crystal."

She reached over, her hand hovering over the scale-covered holder where the crystal was lodged. She yanked it out.

"Hand me another." She waved her fingers.

Marcus grabbed one off the table and set it on her hand.

She jammed it into the holder. More data flashed up. More English.

"Another one," she said.

As they worked through the crystals, Elle muttered to herself. She discarded crystal after crystal in rapid succession.

"Dammit." She yanked another crystal out. "Still only English."

She kept working as Marcus' team prowled around the space. They were getting edgy and so was he.

They'd been here too long.

Their missions were always quick in-out incursions. The raptors knew they were here, somewhere. With a pack of hungry canids out front, it wouldn't take much to find them.

"Come on, Elle," Marcus growled.

"I'm working as fast as I can," she snapped.

He heard the tremor buried under the snark and he gripped her shoulder. "I know you are. You can do this."

She sucked in a deep breath, nodded. "Put in another one, please."

Only Elle would still be using her manners in the middle of a post-apocalyptic warzone. He shoved another crystal in. A few seconds later, she shook her head.

Thumps echoed from the front of the library. They all swiveled to look in that direction. The distant howls of the canids reached them.

"Marcus, we need to go, *amigo,*" Cruz said, shifting his grip on his carbine.

"We aren't leaving without the damn crystal." He put another one into the system, then tapped his earpiece. "Noah?"

Still nothing.

"Get some cover between us and them. Gabe, scout for a secondary exit."

Gabe gave a brief nod before he disappeared into the shadows. The others tipped over some tables and dragged them over.

Marcus and Elle worked through three more crystals before she gasped. "Yes!"

Raptor language filled the screen with its distinctive letters that looked like claw marks and scratches. Elle's eyes moved back and forth as she scanned it.

"Is it enough?" he asked.

She nodded. "I think so."

A crash sounded from the front of the library. The excited yips of the canids sounded—loud and getting louder.

"Time to go." Marcus helped Elle shove the crystal into her backpack. Gripping her bicep, he tugged her close. "Hell Squad, let's get out of here."

***

Elle hurried alongside Marcus, jogging to keep up with his long stride.

The flush of excitement at finding a crystal containing the raptor language had faded in an instant. The howls of the canids sent chills across her skin.

Gabe loomed ahead. "This way."

They maneuvered through the rows of books. Paper books had long ago gone out of favor, eventually becoming nothing more than quaint collectibles. But the invasion had made them popular again in the base. Not everyone had a working portable comp, so they had to read from paper. She spared one longing glance at the shelves and shelves of books before focusing on their escape. She needed all her concentration to keep up with Hell Squad and not slow them down.

Gabe opened a side door to the outside. He slipped out with his gun up, followed by Claudia.

"It's clear," Gabe said.

They stepped out into a deserted alley, parts of it in shadow as the sun sank toward the west. Large plastic waste containers were lined up near the door, some marked for trash, others for recycling. To the left was a dead end, dominated by an overflowing dumpster that stank of rot.

Shaw cursed. He had a palm pressed to the now-closed door. "It's self-locking. We can't go back that way."

Marcus nodded. "Doesn't matter." They moved together in a tight formation, headed toward the entrance on the right. "We need to—"

Suddenly, a team of seven enormous raptors appeared at the alley entrance.

Elle gasped. They were so big, and all brandishing wicked-looking weapons that vaguely resembled Hell Squad's carbines, but were covered in scales. She heard Marcus curse.

Then the raptors opened fire.

Marcus shoved Elle back hard, and she fell behind the waste containers. She stayed there for a second on her hands and knees. Dark-green poison splattered the wall above her. The roar of her squad's carbines was loud in her ears as their neon green laser fire lit up the alley. She heard Marcus calling orders to his team.

She lifted her head and risked a glance. Saw the raptors advancing and Marcus and others returning fire.

They were trapped in this damn alley like animals in a cage.

She pulled out her thermo pistol and tried to calm her racing heart. Marcus was right, this was way worse than listening to a fight over the comms.

Then she heard another terrible sound.

Canids growling.

She swiveled. The first dog-like alien came through the door from the library. It was big, the size of a wolf, with a spiked ridge along its back. The animal lifted its head and spotted her.

It opened its mouth, baring sharp teeth. Then it leaped into the air and with one bound, landed on top of the waste container in front of her.

Elle scrambled backward.

And dropped her pistol.

The canid leaned down, its jaws snapping. It smelled like rotting meat and old blood.

Elle moved her hand desperately across the concrete. Her heart was hammering like drums in her chest. *Pistol. Pistol.* She touched cool metal and whipped the gun up…just as the canid leaped at her.

The weapon discharged, the canid's body shuddering under the impact of the thermo bullets. The creature fell on top of her, pinning her to the cracked pavement.

She stayed there for a second, panting. Warm stickiness coated her chest. *Ick*, canid blood. With a heave, she pushed the animal off her.

More raptor poison hit the wall above her head.

With a yelp, she ducked back down, cheek to the ground.

Then Marcus was there, his big body shielding her and pressing her into the ground. He patted a hand over her blood-soaked armor. "Where are you hit? Are you okay?"

She gripped his wrist. "It's not mine. I'm fine."

He spotted the canid's body and his jaw tightened. Then he touched his ear. "Noah? Tell me you got the comms fixed."

"I'm here. I broke through the jamming signal."

Noah's voice was still faint, but clear enough. Elle released a breath.

"We need a way out," Marcus said. "We're pinned in an alley."

"Okay. Okay." Noah sounded harried. He was probably regretting volunteering to do comms. "I've got a Hawk on its way. And I'm searching for an exit for you."

"Now, Noah!" Marcus yelled.

"He'll come through," Elle said. "Noah always comes through."

A distant roar echoed through the alley.

"Shit," Marcus bit off.

Elle swallowed. *Boom. Boom. Boom.* The ground beneath them trembled.

The raptors ahead scrambled out of the way. Two huge, scaled legs with clawed feet the size of SUVs stepped into view.

It took another step and the huge, bulky body of the rex filled the alley entrance.

It lifted its enormous head and roared.

Chapter Eight

In his head, Marcus worked through all the curse words he knew. And he knew a lot.

This was bad. *Fucking bad.*

He stepped closer to Elle and wished like hell she was anywhere but here. He needed to keep her safe. He needed a way out.

She was looking around and he could almost see the wheels turning in her head.

“Marcus. Back through the library. We need to go that way.” She pointed.

He saw the door that had locked behind them was now torn and bent from where the canid had come through.

He cupped the nape of her neck. “Good work.” Then he looked back at the team. “Everyone, back into the library.”

They sprinted toward the door. The raptors opened fire again. The thick, green goo hit the side of the building, sizzling as it ate into the brick. The squad returned fire.

The rex roared again and took a step into the alley. But the massive creature’s progress was halted by the tall buildings on either side of the narrow alley.

As they moved inside, it took Marcus' eyes a second to adjust to the dim light. Elle stumbled on an overturned chair. He grabbed her arm and kept her on her feet. They ran down the rows of shelves.

Suddenly, part of the roof gave way with a crash and a huge clawed foot came down and squashed the bookcase beside them.

Marcus swerved left and looked up. Through the gaping hole in the roof, he saw the rex.

"Marcus." Noah's voice cut through the chaos. "Hawk will be landing in five minutes in a park two blocks north of your location."

"Roger that, Noah. Now keep quiet. We have a hungry rex to deal with." A raptor appeared in front of them. Marcus shot it in the head. "Everyone, keep moving!"

"Marcus!"

Claudia's shout came through the earpiece. Followed by Cruz's swearing in Spanish.

Marcus swiveled. Elle slammed to a stop against his chest.

Hell. Claudia was pinned by an overturned bookcase. Cruz was trying to free her but one of his arms was hanging uselessly by his side and covered in blood and it looked like the bookcase was too heavy even with the help of his armor's exoskeleton.

Three raptors were heading their way, tossing debris out of their path to get to them.

Overhead, the rex roared, smashing its tail through a wall. Hunks of plaster flew through the air, one smacking Marcus in the back. He pulled

Elle to his chest, curling his body around hers.

"Fucking fuck." Shaw appeared beside them. He knelt and sighted his rifle at the raptors bearing down on Cruz and Claudia. "We have to get her out of there."

Gabe rushed passed them, sprinting toward the pair.

"Zeke!" Marcus roared.

The man materialized beside him. He held his carbine in one hand and his knife—covered in raptor blood—in the other. "Boss?"

"You take Elle and you get her out of here. Get to the evac point."

"Marcus, no!" she said. "You need Zeke here."

"I need you safe."

She opened her mouth and he gripped the front of her armor and yanked her onto her toes. He pressed a quick kiss to her open mouth.

"I. Need. You. Safe," he growled.

He didn't wait to see that she followed his order. He spun and plowed toward his fallen team members. Shaw had taken down a raptor, Gabe was wrestling with another. Marcus lifted his carbine and shot the third.

More raptors stormed through the door from the alley.

"Shaw and Gabe, get Claudia and Cruz out." Marcus stepped between his team and the door. "I'll hold them off."

The sniper didn't miss a beat. He leaped to his feet and raced over to Claudia. Gabe followed, then gripped the heavy bookcase with one hand and heaved. It should have been far too heavy for one man to lift, but it moved.

Marcus kept firing his carbine. The front few raptors fell but he knew there were too many. All he had to do was keep the majority of them off his team and give them a chance to escape. Two aliens rushed him.

He went down under the weight of them. As he fell, he yanked out the two gladius combat knives he carried.

God, the raptors were heavy bastards. They were bigger than humans but they were also more dense. He stabbed one up through the ribs, rolling to avoid the second raptor's jagged, black blade.

They strained against each other. The raptor's red eyes were narrowed on Marcus. The alien managed to force Marcus' arms away from him and aim his blade for Marcus' throat.

Fuck. Marcus pushed upward, trying to keep the wicked edge away from his skin.

Suddenly, the rex crashed through the roof again.

Chunks of ceiling crashed on top of Marcus and his opponent.

While the raptor was startled, Marcus jammed his elbow up, catching the creature's chin. With his other hand, he jammed his knife into the softer flesh under the raptor's neck. The skin there was still harder than a human's and Marcus had to work the knife in. Finally, blood spurted and the raptor made an agonized noise.

Marcus heaved the creature off him and rolled

away. He pushed to his feet. As he sprinted to his people, he saw that Gabe had managed to get the bookcase off Claudia and Shaw was helping her up.

The rex roared, a sound so loud it made Marcus' ears ring. He glanced over his shoulder and almost lost his footing.

The rex was staring down through the hole in the roof.

Right at them.

Its red eyes looked like the fires of hell.

"Go! Get her out," Marcus yelled. But he knew it was too late. The rex could kill them all with a single swipe of its claws.

"Hey! Ugly! Over here."

Marcus stumbled, his gut pulling tight. *No. No. No.*

Elle yelled again. "Yeah, come on you hideous thing. Come this way and leave them alone."

Marcus clenched his hands. He saw her on the other side of the library, waving her arms in the air.

He saw the rex tilt its head, watching her.

It had lost interest in the rest of them.

Zeke rushed in beside Marcus. "Sorry, boss. She got away from me and refused to leave without you."

Jaw tight, Marcus moved to the others. "Up and at it, soldier."

"Yes, sir." Claudia grimaced. Shaw was holding her upright. "I can make it."

The rex let out a horrible roar and Marcus watched Elle lunge to the side.

The rex swiped out with its claws.

Marcus' heart just stopped.

Agile and nimble, Elle dropped flat on the floor. The creature's massive claw swiped through the air about a meter above her head.

She leaped back up in one lithe jump and started running. Her gaze caught Marcus'.

Come on, baby. She was running flat-out.

The rex stamped its feet, managing to squash the last few raptors heading Hell Squad's way. Then it swiped at Elle again.

And this time he caught her.

The creature raised its claw, Elle dangling from it, her arms and legs thrashing.

No. Marcus swung his carbine around and ran toward her.

***

Adrenaline stormed through Elle, leaving her heart racing and her mind pumped.

The rex's claws had hooked into the back of her armor. The creature was waving her, wildly trying to shake her loose.

She couldn't see anything but a blur of color, but she heard laser fire.

Then she felt her armor tear a little, dropping her down a few inches. She held her breath. Another shake and her armor ripped on the sharp claw and she tore free of the rex.

She fell several meters to the floor and hit with a hard slap. The air rushed out of her lungs with an *oof*.

Stunned for a second, she stayed sprawled amongst torn-up books and broken shelving, staring at the rex's giant claws.

Hands gripped the back of her armor and yanked her up. She caught a brief glimpse of Marcus' scarily enraged face before she was tossed over his broad shoulder.

Too out of it to speak, she saw of the rest of Hell Squad getting ready to move. Claudia was standing, but favoring one leg, and pointing a finger at Shaw.

"You try and carry me and I'll gut you," Claudia snapped.

"You're hurt—"

"I can walk. The damn exoskeleton in my armor will help."

"You stubborn idiot—"

"Shut your mouth or I'll shut it for you. With my fist."

"Fine. I won't carry you—" he slid an arm around her shoulders and fought her when she tried to pull away "—but I'm helping you out of here. Compromise, Frost. A word you've probably never heard of."

She swore at him.

"Ah, there's your sweet disposition shining through."

"Enough." Marcus jerked his head. "Let's get out of here. Now."

"How'd you get Elle to let you carry her?" Shaw asked as they headed through the library.

"I didn't give her a choice."

"Don't even think about it," Claudia snapped.

Elle cleared her throat. "Marcus, I can walk."

He ignored her.

Moments later, they exited out the front door of the library. The team hurried down the street. Elle braced her hands on Marcus' back to stop bouncing all over the place. He was all rock-hard muscle under her palms.

The sun was headed rapidly toward the western horizon and the shadows were growing. She swallowed the lump in her throat. They did *not* want to be here once dark hit. She'd heard rumors of alien beasts that only came out at night and left nothing behind but bones picked clean of flesh.

They moved along the street, Gabe and Zeke ahead, weapons up.

Then she heard the canids.

Elle swiveled her head and saw the pack running at full speed, leaping over anything in their path. God, they never gave up.

Cruz stopped and swiveled. He pulled a grenade from his belt, armed it and tossed it with his good arm toward the canids.

The creatures suddenly started howling, some dropping to the ground, their heads between their paws. Others turned in circles, disoriented.

Elle frowned. She hadn't seen an explosion?

"Sonic grenade," Marcus said.

But a few of the canids made it through, their mouths open, teeth bared.

"Fuck." Cruz scrambled to get his carbine aimed.

Suddenly, a black bolt whistled though the air and slammed through the head of the lead canid. The animal dropped, tripping the canid behind it.

More bolts came in quick succession. One, two, three.

The canids at the back of the group skidded to a halt, wary. By then, Gabe and Zeke were in position and laid down a barrage of laser fire.

Cruz stood still, his gaze searching the rooftops. Elle swiveled enough to get a quick glimpse of a lean figure leaping between two buildings. Then the figure was gone, swallowed by the shadows.

"Let's go!" Marcus barked, jostling her.

Elle watched Cruz scan the buildings once more before he cursed and ran to the closest dead canid. He yanked out the bolt, then ran back to join the group.

Moving at a fast jog, it didn't take long before Elle saw trees and waist-high grass.

She felt a rush of air and she was suddenly flipped over and set on her feet. Ahead, the quadcopter was coming in to land.

Gabe leaped up first and helped Cruz up. Shaw and Zeke helped a scowling Claudia onto the copter. Next, Marcus handed Elle up to Gabe.

As soon as Marcus climbed aboard, the Hawk lifted off.

She heard the distant roar of the rex as the copter turned and headed toward the setting sun.

Shaw started checking a protesting Claudia's leg while Gabe tore open a first-aid kit and wrapped a white bandage around Cruz's bleeding arm.

Marcus stood, one hand gripping the handholds above his head, staring at the floor. His other hand was held in a tight fist at his side.

Elle sat on the edge of the chair and swallowed. She wasn't an idiot. She felt the rage pulsing off him. She caught Shaw's gaze. He gave her a wink, but she saw sympathy swimming in his eyes.

"Are you hurt?"

The rasp of Marcus' voice was so low she barely heard him. His tone was so icy-cold it sent a violent shiver through her.

"No. The rex just ripped my armor—"

Marcus spun, his green eyes blazing. "What the fuck did you think you were doing?"

Elle opened her mouth. Closed it. She couldn't seem to make any words come out. Funny that she felt more afraid now than she had when the rex was shaking her around like a toy. She cleared her throat. "Saving you. And the others."

"By making yourself rex bait?"

Cruz stirred. "Marcus—"

"Shut it, Cruz."

Marcus strode forward until Elle found her nose pressed to his body armor.

"Never again," he ground out. "No more missions. No more wrestling with canids. No more rexes even a mile near you."

The air caught in her chest. "Marcus—"

He snatched her into his arms. "Be quiet." He sank down at the back of the copter, his back to the wall, his arms wrapped tightly around her. "Don't say anything because I'm too fucking angry." He rested his chin on top of her head and pulled her tight against him. "I've got more to say…back at base."

Elle caught Claudia's gaze. The other woman looked like she was trying to smother a smile. Elle didn't know what she found so funny.

Elle tried again. "Marcus—"

He moved his head so his lips were pressed against her ear. His deep voice was pitched only for her to hear. "Quiet. Otherwise I'll strip those fatigues off you, turn you over my knee and spank you right here."

She knew her eyes must be bugging out of her head. And it had to be so, so wrong that she felt a rush of warmth through her belly. Even with the fury pulsating off him, and his very intimate threat, she knew he'd never hurt her.

She settled back against him and figured she may as well enjoy the feel of being in his arms.

Because who knew what she'd have to deal with once they got back to base.

Chapter Nine

As the Hawk descended onto the landing pads, Marcus still felt fury surging through his blood stream in a molten rush.

He kept seeing Elle clutched in the rex's claws and reflexively, his arms tightened around her. How easily she could have been snuffed out. What would he fight for then?

Finn, the Hawk pilot, leaned back from the cockpit, his blond hair almost brushing his shoulders. The man was magic with the quadcopters. "Welcome home, Hell Squad. Always a pleasure."

Zeke groaned. "Happy to be home. I need a shower, a beer and a woman." He grimaced and shot a glance at Elle. "Sorry, Ellie."

She smiled. "Like I haven't already heard all kinds of stories about you and your…charm."

Marcus surged to his feet, bringing Elle with him. "Okay, we need to get Cruz and Claudia to the infirmary."

Shaw was already helping Claudia up. As soon as she put weight on her leg, her face went white.

"Fuck it." Shaw scooped her into his arms.

"Asshole," she snapped. "You wouldn't carry

Cruz or Gabe around. Put me down—"

"Just shut it, Frost." He leaped out of the Hawk.

Cruz's dark gaze snagged Marcus. He lifted the crossbow bolt. "Who do you think our mystery savior was?"

Marcus shrugged. "Someone still holed up in the city."

Cruz stroked the sleek, black bolt. "Can't be a civilian. Not with aim that good. And this is homemade, tipped with explosive and excellent quality."

"How about you worry about your arm for now?" Marcus could see Cruz had lost a lot of blood.

Cruz tossed him a sloppy salute, one he knew drove Marcus crazy. "Yes, Staff Sergeant."

Gabe helped Cruz out of the Hawk. Outside, Marcus saw Doc Emerson rush up.

"Who else is in need of my fabulous bedside manner? Claudia is already on her way to my domain and bitching every step of the way." Emerson tossed her head, her blonde hair brushing her jaw.

"Cruz injured his arm. Possible break and severe blood loss," Marcus said.

She nodded, then looked at Gabe. "You're all right?"

Always a man of few words, Gabe gave one curt nod.

The doctor released a breath. "Okay. Come on, Cruz, let me stick some tiny robots in you and probably a whole lot of needles."

Cruz rolled his eyes. "Great."

With his team taken care of, Marcus had one more thing that needed his attention. He leaped off the Hawk and as soon as his boots hit the ground, he reached for Elle.

She hesitated, her face more than a little wary.

Good. So she should be. He grabbed her around the waist and tossed her over his shoulder. She let out a squeak.

He strode toward the entrance to the tunnel leading to his quarters.

"Marcus, put me—"

He slapped a hand over her butt and she huffed out a breath.

"You know, this alpha macho behavior isn't—"

He swatted her butt again. "You should stop talking.

Holmes stepped in front of Marcus. Noah stood beside him, his interested gaze on Elle. Or rather, Elle's rear end. Marcus glared and the other man looked away.

"Glad you and Squad Six got back safely, Steele. You've got the crystal?"

Marcus tugged Elle's backpack free and held it out.

As soon as Holmes took it, Marcus stepped around him and continued on.

"Where are you going?" The general called out. "We need to debrief the mission." He cleared his throat. "And why are you carrying Elle? Is she hurt?"

Marcus half turned. "I'm going to my quarters. We'll debrief in a few hours. And no, Elle isn't hurt.

No thanks to her own stupidity."

Now she came to life, lifting her head. "Stupidity?" She thumped her fist against his back. "I saved your life, you ungrateful—"

Marcus caught Holmes' gaze. "We done?"

The man's usual dignified mask cracked for a second, a half smile on his lips. "Okay. We'll debrief in two hours."

"Three." Marcus was planning to put every single minute of them to good use.

He stalked through the tunnels, ignoring the wide-eyed looks from the people he passed.

He slammed a palm against his door lock, waited for it to beep, then strode inside. He thrust the door closed hard enough to rattle the hinges. His room was cool and dim. After a year, he'd almost gotten used to the lack of windows and the constant whoosh of the air-conditioning.

After setting Elle down, he turned on the small lamp beside the bunk. It cast a warm glow across the room.

Elle stood there, her arms by her sides, the light turning her skin golden.

He started undoing the fastenings on her armor. He loosened the chest armor then tore off the front panel. He tossed it over his shoulder into the floor.

"What are you doing?" she whispered.

"Shh."

She huffed out a breath. "I'm getting pretty sick of you telling me to be quiet."

He ignored her and eased the back panel off. He saw where the ultra-tough composite had been warped and ripped by the rex. He clenched his jaw and rubbed a thumb over the jagged tear.

She sighed. "Marcus, I'm not hurt."

He kept working, pulling all the armor off. Next, he gripped her simple black shirt by the neckline with both hands and ripped it apart. Buttons scattered across the polished concrete floor.

"That cost me two months of clothing credits!"

He knelt and undid her fatigue trousers and slipped them down her shapely legs. It left her standing there in just a plain black bra and panties.

Jesus. His cock went hard in an instant. She was all slim limbs and smooth skin. But he clamped down on his desire. First he had to satisfy this driving need to know—to see with his own eyes—that she was okay.

He circled her fine wrists and ran his hands up her arms. The scrape of his calluses on her skin made him wish they weren't so rough. He cupped the balls of her shoulders, then slid one hand down her back, between her shoulder blades, feeling the delicate knobs of her spine.

Her breath hitched. "What are you doing?" Her voice was thick.

"I'm making sure for myself that you're not injured." He moved his hand back up to grip the delicate stem of her neck. "Such a strong, courageous woman in such a fragile package."

Her eyelids fluttered. Her skin was so pale he could see the blue of her veins beneath, the flutter of the pulse in her neck.

"I'm not fragile."

He almost smiled at the bite in her voice. "I didn't mean it that way. I mean you're so much softer than my hard, scarred body." He ran a finger over her bare shoulder. "So much better."

She raised a hand and cupped his cheek. "You are a good man, Marcus Steele. I won't let anyone say differently. Even you."

Marcus stared into her beautiful blue eyes. "Elle, I'm not—"

"You be quiet now." She lifted her other hand. "You go out there every day and risk your life."

"Because I'm good at killing."

She made a scoffing noise. "You're a good leader, who always puts his team first. Who goes into combat time and again to give humanity's survivors a fighting chance."

"Have you seen my face? It sure as hell isn't pretty." He looked down and saw his blood-covered hands resting on her skin. "Shit, I'm still covered in blood." He pulled them back. "Sometimes I think it doesn't matter how hard I scrub, they'll never be clean."

Her face softened. She stroked a finger over his knuckles. "And sometimes I think I'll never be anything but a frivolous, useless society girl who thinks of no one but herself." She looked away. "You would have hated who I was before."

He gripped her shoulders. "Bullshit. You're the best damn comms officer a squad could ever have. And you think of *everybody* but yourself."

A small smile tilted her lips. "Guess we'll both

have to learn to see ourselves through the other's eyes."

He stared at his tanned, scarred hand resting under hers. "I shouldn't be touching you. I've been trying to stay away from you for months."

"You have?" She pressed her palms against the armor on his chest. "Why?"

"You're too good for me."

"I don't believe that." She raised up on her tiptoes and pressed a kiss to his mouth. "Well, I'll just have to show you how bad I can be."

Marcus groaned and yanked her up. He closed his mouth over hers. He knew the kiss was too hard, too hungry, too raw, but she pressed harder against him, making mewling noises in her throat.

And she kissed him back like she couldn't get enough of him. Her fingers had slid under his armor at the neck, her thumbs stroking his skin.

He pulled back. "Shit. I'm getting raptor blood all over you."

"I already have dried canid blood everywhere." Her hands went to the fastenings of his armor. "Let's get this off you, and then why don't we both get clean?"

Shit. His cock leaped, not just at her words but at the undiluted desire in her eyes. Elle naked and wet in his shower… "The water'll be cold."

She smiled. "Right now, I couldn't possibly feel cold."

***

Elle pulled off the last piece of Marcus' armor and set it aside. Underneath he wore black cargo trousers and an olive-green T-shirt.

He gripped the neck of his shirt and ripped it over his head.

The air left Elle's lungs in a wild rush. He was so…hard.

His broad shoulders were roped in muscle and his stomach was hard ridge after hard ridge. He looked like he was sculpted from granite. His dark skin was crisscrossed with scars. Nothing neat or faint. These were rough and ugly, the badges of courage for a soldier. She touched one, an uneven starburst near his right shoulder. She traced another long, ragged scar that cut down his side.

He stepped back and with a flick of his wrist, undid his cargo trousers and pushed them off.

Now her mouth went dry. She'd dreamed so many times of Marcus naked before her. There was more heavy muscle in his solid, powerful thighs. And a thick—very thick—cock rose up, rock hard.

"Come on," he rasped and pushed her toward the tiny adjoining bathroom.

His bathroom looked like hers. Small, but functional with a white sink under a mirror and a small shower stall done in faded green tiles. Marcus slid back the shower door and flicked on the water.

He helped her strip off her underwear and urged her in. Elle tipped her face up to the spray. Thankfully it wasn't too cold yet, but still only lukewarm at best. Regardless, it felt good to wash the blood and grime away. She felt her muscles relax one by one.

Then Marcus squeezed into the stall behind her.

Now she didn't feel relaxed at all.

He was so big and the shower was so small. His large, hot body pressed against the back of hers. His hard cock brushed the cleft of her bottom and she shivered.

The water fell over them and he reached around and squirted some soap from the dispenser.

Then he started rubbing it over her arms, her shoulders, her back. She knew he was scrubbing away the canid blood.

"Sorry, my soap doesn't smell like flowers like whatever you usually use."

God, he'd noticed what she smelled like. Her heart did a tiny flutter. No, his soap didn't smell like hers. It smelled like Marcus. Something simple, clean, with a hint of musk.

He kept scrubbing. "So wrong to see alien blood on this skin." His hands slipped into her hair, lathering it. "And this hair..." He worked the soap into the strands, lifting the wet mass off the back of her neck "I've had dreams about all this hair."

Elle shivered and let her head drop back against his shoulder. "I've dreamed of more than your hair."

He let out a short laugh. "I've dreamed of you naked in my bed—hell, naked *anywhere*—since the first moment I saw you."

She stilled. "You've wanted me since then?"

"Yes. Those big, blue eyes watching me. I figured

you must have been scared to death of me."

She smiled. "Hardly. I was mesmerized. You were so big, strong…maybe a little intimidating. But I've never been scared of you. You're a protector, Marcus. Anyone—man, woman or child—knows that the instant they see you."

He leaned down and nipped the side of her neck. Just rough enough to excite. She gasped.

"But what if you need protection from *me*?"

As he kissed her neck, teeth scraping in the most erotic way, his soapy hands slipped down and cupped her breasts.

She cried out, arching into his touch.

"You like that?" He flicked his fingers over her nipples. "These are beautiful breasts, Elle. Not too big, not too small. Perfect."

God, she wanted to touch him, but he kept her caged with his big body, touching her all over with those slick hands. The glide of wet skin against wet skin was intoxicating. His hands slid lower, sliding down her belly, leaving her quivering.

One hand slipped between her legs. His fingers grazed across her clit and her hips rocked into his touch, a whimper coming from her throat.

"I know, baby." He explored her with a soft, teasing caress. He ran his finger through her folds.

She whimpered again. "More."

A masculine chuckle. "Greedy girl." His finger touched her clit.

He rubbed and her legs went weak. He kept caressing her with firm, slick circles.

He held her up, and pleasure was a wild,

growing warmth that was taking her over. God, she needed to come. The water, much cooler now, continued to pour over their heads. It was just the two of them, locked together, Elle straining against Marcus. There was no one else in the world but them and the pleasure.

"Enough," he growled and flicked off the water.

Startled, Elle blinked. "I'm so close—"

"I know, baby. But the first time I make you come, I want it to be around my cock."

His words made her lower body spasm.

He pushed her out of the shower and didn't bother with a towel. He scooped her up, and in a few quick strides reached his bunk. He dropped her onto the covers. "I can't wait any longer. Got to be inside you."

The sheets smelled like him—dark and masculine. He knelt beside the bed, his strong hands sliding up her thighs.

"So damn beautiful." He stroked a hand over her stomach, a finger playing with the dark curls at the juncture of her thighs.

Elle's eyelids fluttered and she bit her lip. She was going to combust if he didn't do something, anything, soon. "Touch me."

He slid one thick finger inside her. She reared up, crying out.

"That's it, baby." He worked his finger inside her, his thumb putting glorious pressure on her clit.

Sensation was a raw, primal electricity running through every nerve in her body. The slippery edge of release was rising up to meet her and she wanted to go over. So badly.

"No." His thumb moved away and he leaned down and sucked a nipple into his mouth.

"Marcus!"

"You aren't coming without me inside you. So deep you feel every inch of me."

Another spasm rocked her. "*Yes.*" She wanted him inside her too.

He lapped at her breast, then pulled back. His finger slipped out of her and then he was gripping her hips and dragging her to the side of the bed. He pushed her knees up and out, opening her to him.

Elle had the fleeting thought she should be embarrassed, but the hungry look on his face just made her feel hot and wanted.

He circled his cock with one hand, pumped it once, then pressed it between her open legs. He circled her entrance with the thick head.

Elle was panting. She needed him so badly. "I'm so empty, Marcus. Fill me up."

With a groan, he reared up and slid inside her with one hard thrust.

Her cry echoed through the small room. He was so thick, and he stretched her hard. A pleasure-pain that pushed her right to the edge.

He planted his hands either side of her on the bed and started moving. "Can't go slow this time, Elle."

She wound her legs around his waist. "I don't want slow."

He moved faster, his hard thrusts thumping her

into the bed. The intense look on his rough face took her breath away.

Her orgasm built so fast, she wasn't ready for it. Her hands twisted in the sheets and then all the feeling in her exploded. She screamed his name, her hips jerking up.

He leaned over her. Slick skin against slick skin. He didn't pause in his hard thrusts.

He didn't give her a chance to relax or come down. His big body kept powering inside hers.

"Again," he growled.

Oh, God. "I…I can't." She'd never come more than once with any other lover, and sometimes she never came at all, unless she did the job herself.

"Yes, you can." He gripped her hips, tilting them. It made him slide deeper and she moaned. "With me this time."

He kept moving, the new angle igniting something inside her. Incredibly, she felt a second orgasm building, faster and more intense than the first.

She moaned, her body shivering. Her hands grabbed at his shoulders, her nails scoring his skin as she tried to find some anchor in the chaos.

Then her release slammed into her. *Sweet oblivion.*

A second later, he dragged her closer and thrust into her to the hilt. He held himself there, groaning as his release hit and he poured himself inside her.

Marcus dropped onto the bed beside her and pulled her into the curve of his body. Elle wasn't sure she'd ever be able to move again. Her body felt light and heavy at the same time.

She pressed her lips to his damp shoulder.

He kissed her temple. "Never, ever risk yourself again."

Her insides went warm. "Marcus."

"Never again." He tugged her closer and buried his face in her hair.

Chapter Ten

Marcus tightened his arms around Elle. She was here, in his bunk, naked, his seed drying on her thighs.

Nothing had ever felt so right.

"I can't promise never to risk myself," she said quietly. "The world's gone to hell, Marcus. We all have to fight to survive."

Her words cut through his gut. He felt a driving need to protect her, from everything. But he knew she was right, dammit. In the ruin of the Earth, all of them had to fight.

"You do it from the Comms Control Room."

Her fingers brushed the stubble on his cheek, stroking. "I hate knowing you're out there, fighting. I have to hear it all, my mind imagining every gun shot, every raptor bearing down on you."

He gripped her hand. "It's what I'm trained for. Baby, you promise me you'll never pull a stunt like you did with that rex again."

Her blue eyes flashed. "I'd do it again if I had to."

Marcus sighed. He loved her courage as much as her quiet intelligence and her gorgeous body. But he never, ever wanted to relive that moment with the rex again. "Then you deserve your punishment."

She raised up on her elbow, her eyes wide. "Punishment?"

He sat and pulled her over his lap. "Told you I'd have to spank you."

"You can't be serious!" She squirmed, trying to get away.

He held her still with one hand on her lower back. "I want you safe, Elle. Even from yourself." Jesus, the creamy curves of her ass taunted him. He gave her a light tap with his open palm.

She jerked. "Marcus!"

He liked the contrast of his big, darker hand against her pale skin. He slapped her other cheek.

She squealed and he knew he didn't have it in him to cause her any real pain. He caressed the soft globe, marveling at how smooth her skin was.

When she moved against him, pushing up into his palm, he paused. "You like it?"

She looked back over her shoulder, her face flushed. "No, I love it. I like you touching me. In any way."

"Good." She loved his touch. Him, a rough, crude soldier. "Because I love touching you. But I don't want to spank this delectable ass." He caressed her bottom again, running a finger between her cheeks and down until he slid into her tight, wet heat.

"Oh." She moved into his touch. "That's so good."

He thrust his finger in and out, then slid a second one inside her. She ground down against his lap and no doubt she felt his cock against her hip, hard as steel.

Marcus pulled her up, swiveling her to face him, her legs straddling him. "I didn't ask you about protection."

"It's okay—"

"No. It's not. I said I'd protect you, so I should have thought of it. I have a contraceptive implant and I'm healthy."

She cupped his cheek with one hand. "Good. And I'm healthy, too."

He released a breath. All the soldiers had contraceptive implants that lasted several years, but he wasn't sure what would happen when they ran out. He had heard Emerson was trying to replicate the implants, but hadn't had any success so far.

Then Elle moved and all sensible thoughts rushed out of his head.

With a smile, she raised her hips, and reached down and circled his cock. Her gaze never leaving his, she sank down, taking every each of him inside her.

"God." The word exploded between his gritted teeth.

She smiled, a temptress out to seduce him. Then she lifted her hips and began to ride him.

"Elle." He slid his hands into her hair. "You make everything worthwhile."

She rode him hard with her breasts bobbing, her breath coming in hard pants. He lifted his hips to meet her and she kept moving until she came, her body shuddering above him. Then he slammed her down and emptied himself inside her.

As he pulled her close and lifted the covers over them, she curled into him and he felt something settle inside him. Something that had been angry and eating at him for so long.

He pressed a kiss to her lips. "Sleep. I have to head out to see Holmes soon, but I'll be back as soon as I can."

She mumbled something and kissed him back, her eyelids already closed.

The debrief with Holmes took close to two hours. Marcus was itching to get back to Elle and, for once, he and the general avoided their usual fireworks. Holmes had a stick up his ass and loved the rules, but Marcus couldn't argue that the man didn't have the best interests of the base's varied inhabitants at heart.

Marcus strode back toward his quarters, trying not to give in to the urge to jog and get there faster. At his door, he pressed his palm to the lock and it opened quietly.

He crept into the room, but it only took him a moment to realize Elle wasn't sleeping peacefully like he'd hoped.

The sheets were twisted around her slim legs and she was tossing and turning.

Marcus sat on the edge of the bed and touched her shoulder. "Elle?"

She jerked upright with a sob.

"Hey." He gripped her shoulders. In the dim light, he could see her eyes were confused, still fogged by her nightmare. "Elle?"

She blinked. "Marcus?" Her voice was jagged.

He stroked the hair off her face. "Nightmare about the rex?"

She dragged in a jerky breath. "I wish."

He waited her out, just stroking her hair.

"About the invasion," she whispered.

He frowned. "You have it a lot?"

She curled her arms around herself. "Every night." A toneless whisper. "I'm trapped in the dark. I can hear the raptors coming. Their grunts, heavy footsteps, noisy breathing." She started shaking. "I'm so afraid. Hiding in the closet in my room. Then I hear my mother scream." A sob broke free from Elle's throat. "My father shouting."

Marcus tugged her into his arms, she struggled against him.

"I did nothing." Her eyes were wild, tears slipping down her cheeks. "I hid like a coward, too afraid and too weak to help them."

"Elle—"

"I heard them die, Marcus. I just looked out for myself and I let them die."

"It wasn't your fault."

She shook her head. "Nothing I do can ever make up for it. I was useless."

He shook her a little. "You aren't useless and none of us are the same people we were before. And the *raptors* killed your parents, not you. What could you have done? Would getting yourself killed really have helped?"

He saw something flicker in her eyes, but then she pulled in on herself.

Enough. He yanked her forward and kissed her.

He tugged her head back with a hand tangled in her hair. "Not your fault." He didn't have any soft words in him. He could only help her with the raw desire that burned inside him. Help her realize that she was alive and it was okay to live.

He pushed her onto her back. "Knees up, Elle. Spread your legs."

She watched him intently, her gaze never leaving his face. Thankfully, the tears had stopped.

Slowly, she pulled her knees up and let them fall apart.

"Good girl." God, she was all pretty and pink and open for him. He leaned down and pressed a kiss to her hip bone. She shifted under his lips. "Stay still," he warned.

He moved down and pressed his mouth to her.

He didn't give her time to think, just licked and sucked. Shit, she tasted so damn good. A sweet, honey taste he wanted to enjoy every day of his life.

"Marcus." She tried to press up into him, but he held her down. He used his tongue on her before finding her clit and sucking it.

With a scream, she imploded, her husky cries sweet sounds in his ears.

He got to his feet and jerked his clothes off. Then he flipped her over. "On your knees."

He wasn't going to give her time to think and brood. He wanted her only to feel.

She moved, thrusting the sweet curves of her butt back against him. Marcus swallowed a groan, fisted his cock with one hand and gripped her hip with the other, his fingers digging into her skin.

Then he thrust forward and slid inside her.

They both groaned. Damn, she was so hot and wet, like a tight glove around him. He bent over her and pressed a kiss to her neck.

"I'm going to take you hard. I can't be gentle right now. I need you."

"Yes." She pushed back against him.

He slid out and slammed back in. "I want you to feel me long after I'm gone." Another hard thrust.

"Marcus!"

He found a fast rhythm that had sensations coiling at the base of his spine. "When you sit in your chair in the control room, you'll be sore and still feeling me."

"Yes!"

He pressed a palm to the small of her back, holding her in place for his relentless thrusts. She made husky cries and moved into him.

Then she screamed and started coming. Her body clamped down on his cock, her inner muscles tightening around him, and he groaned. Seconds later, he came in a long, hard rush, throwing his head back as the sensation roared through him.

She fell onto the bed in a boneless sprawl, her dark hair in disarray. He nudged her aside and leaned over her. Her eyelids were closed. Fast asleep.

With a smile, he lay down beside her and tugged her close. Damn, she felt right in his arms. The perfect fit. He thought of her having that nightmare over and over… He'd make it his own personal mission to make sure she slept well every night.

But as he stared at the ceiling, his smile dissolved. He had to remember that she was still finding herself, discovering her confidence and the new her in this crazy, changed world.

One day, she'd wake up and wonder why she'd ever let a rough, battle-scarred grunt like him close.

But that day wasn't today. So for now, she was his and he was going to enjoy the hell out of her.

***

As Elle entered the dining room at Marcus' side, she felt like everyone was watching them.

She lifted her chin. Let them look. Gossip in the tight confines of the base was rife. It was a fact of life. Besides, she didn't care if they talked about the fact she had stubble burn on her cheeks and neck—and in a few other sensitive places they wouldn't get to see.

She was proud as hell she'd driven a man like Marcus to the wild desire he'd shown her. She'd had a decent enough love life before the invasion, or she'd thought she had. She'd believed she'd known what sex was all about. But Marcus had blown that all away. Making love with him had been…she drew in an unsteady breath…*amazing*.

“There are the guys.” Marcus directed her toward a table with a hand at the small of her back.

That slight touch made her shiver and a few places inside her light up.

He glanced down, his lips twitching. "I just spent all night fucking you senseless. You can't be ready again."

She licked her lips. "It seems when it comes to you, I can."

Fire ignited in his eyes. "Later." His voice was thick.

As they passed a table, Elle saw Liberty sitting with some friends. The blonde eyed her, then Marcus, then gave Elle a thumbs-up and a wink.

All of Hell Squad sat at the end of one of the long trestle tables lined up in the room. Noah was with them. They were all watching as Marcus and Elle approached.

Claudia's dark eyes shifted between the two of them. "Thank fuck."

Shaw grinned. "Nice work, boss."

"About damn time." Cruz lifted a piece of toast and took a bite.

"Shut it," Marcus growled as he pulled a chair out for Elle.

Elle's face was on fire, but she tried to ignore it. "Claudia? Cruz? You're okay?"

Claudia stuck her leg out to the side. "Good as new." She tilted her head. "Thanks for keeping that rex off us."

Elle felt Marcus tense beside her and winced. "Don't mention it." She dipped her head toward Marcus. "Really, don't. Marcus is still a bit…touchy about it."

As Claudia snorted and the guys laughed, Marcus rattled her chair. “Sit. I’ll grab us a couple of plates.”

She smiled her thanks and sat. Then she watched him head over to the food tables and got caught staring at the way his cargo trousers cupped what she now knew was one tight, muscled butt. And the way his T-shirt stretched over his chest, leaving those heavy biceps on display. Strong arms that lifted her so easily, and were so sturdy as they held her in place for his thrusts—

“So, you and Marcus, huh?”

Noah’s voice intruded, startling her out of her fantasy. She turned. “Yes.”

“Would never have pegged it.”

She smiled. “He’s the most amazing man I’ve ever known.”

Noah studied her face, then shook his head. “No one else ever had a chance, did they?”

She saw something in his eyes. *Oh, God.* “Noah…I never realized—”

He shrugged. “I like you, Elle. You’re smart and sweet. I took too long to make a move.” He shot her a wry smile. “I’m not that great with the whole emotions thing. And tossing you over my shoulder isn’t really my style.”

“I consider you a friend, Noah.”

“I know. Me, too.” He touched her hand. “Friends. I’m happy for you. Marcus might be rough around the edges, but the guy’s a goddamn hero.”

Marcus returned and set a plate down in front of

Elle. She eyed the mound of food incredulously. Marcus might be able to pack that away but there was no chance she'd be able to.

He sat in the chair beside her and picked up his fork. He glanced at Noah. "Any progress on the crystal?"

"Not much. I had to rework the cradle I'd devised to interface the crystal to our computers. It's fascinating technology. I still haven't worked out how the raptors have manipulated the crystalline structure of the…" Noah trailed off. "I just geeked on you, didn't I?"

"Uh-huh." Marcus took a bite of his substitute eggs.

"Right. Well, I finished modifying the cradle I'm using to link the crystals into our systems. Before I came down here to find you guys, I plugged the crystal in and pulled off some data." He grinned. "English and raptor."

Elle smiled at Marcus. He smiled back.

They ate for a while and she listened to Claudia and Shaw sniping at each other. Elle was reminded of how close the squad was. They were like their own little family unit.

"You know, I could use your help, Elle," Noah said, interrupting her musings. "You're better at raptor than me."

"Sure. I can't eat any more anyway." She nudged her plate away. "You want to start now?"

Noah nodded. He grabbed their plates and headed to the wash-up area.

Elle stood and suddenly felt nervous. Marcus

hadn't showed any overt affection in public. He probably wouldn't want her to make a scene. Should she touch him, though?

"Um, I'll see you later." She hated feeling uncertain around him.

Marcus suddenly grabbed her, yanked her into his lap, and kissed her.

All thoughts of etiquette flew out of her head. She cupped his rough cheeks and kissed him back.

The catcalls and whistles faded away. There was just Marcus and the delicious taste and feel of him.

When he set her back on her feet, she felt a bit dazed.

"Later," he said. "I'll be in the gym, sparring with Cruz, if you need me."

She blinked, trying to get her brain to function normally. "Right. Okay."

He smiled at her and because she couldn't help herself, she traced his jaw. "Bye." She tossed a wave at the rest of Hell Squad who, she noticed, were all grinning like idiots.

Chapter Eleven

Elle had been staring at the screen so long she'd given herself a headache. So many of the glowing raptor symbols mocked her, refusing to give up their meanings. She slammed a palm against her desk. She kept seeing the same symbols in different combinations that made no sense.

She rubbed at her temple and shifted in her seat. She felt some unfamiliar aches in a few intimate places. That made her smile and her thoughts turned instantly to Marcus. Even though he'd kept her very busy most of the night, she'd also had the best sleep she'd had since the aliens attacked. Held tight in his arms, she felt safe, protected.

Looking back at the screen, she focused on what she *had* learned. The aliens called themselves the Gizzida.

And this wasn't the first time they'd invaded a planet, destroyed its leadership, and then taken everything they wanted.

If her translations were correct, they were from the Alphard star system, part of the Hydra constellation. She sank back in her chair. It was appropriate since Hydra was a snake. Even the research on Alphard, an orange giant star, showed an uncanny link to the aliens—the Arabs had called it "backbone of the serpent." To the Chinese it was "red bird" and one famous European astronomer had called it "heart of the snake." She tapped in a command and sent her latest report through to General Holmes.

It was all very interesting but it didn't help find the hub.

She reached for the mug of coffee Noah had brought her before he'd headed off…somewhere. She took a swig and nearly spat it everywhere. It was stone cold.

"Ugh." She pushed it aside and stared at the screen again.

She eyed the notes she'd made on her tablet. She'd translated a few words but these next symbols had her stuck.

Scribbling on the tablet, she tried a few word combinations but nothing made sense. She sighed and rubbed her blurry eyes. She *had* to find the location of that comms hub. She straightened her shoulders and stared again at the screen.

Suddenly it went blank.

She shot to the edge of her chair. "What the hell?"

"Time for a break." Marcus stepped into view holding up an unplugged cable.

"Marcus, you can't do that! I'm getting close but I still have a bunch of words I need to decipher. Every time I think I have it, they seem to change—"

"No. *Break.*"

She stood and faced off with him. "This from the man who I know usually spends all his free time monitoring drone feed, assessing raptor strategy and planning missions. We need to find that hub—"

"You won't find it if you work yourself into the ground. You've been here for eight hours straight and you worked through lunch."

"Eight hours?" *Oh.* Where had the time gone?

"Food. Rest. Relaxation." His tone was the same one he used to order his team around.

She bristled. "I'm not one of your soldiers."

He leaned down, his mouth hovering over hers. "No, I'm the man who had his cock inside you last night. The man who wants to take care of you and the man who'd like to hold you in his arms again for a little while."

The air rushed out of her lungs and a warm glow filled her chest. "What did you have in mind?"

"A sunset picnic."

As he tugged her from the computer lab, Elle tried to process what he'd just said. Sunset picnics and rugged Marcus Steele did not go together. Ever. Not even in her wildest fantasies.

He led her through various tunnels and into a less-used part the base. Most of the rooms here were used for storage of supplies. Eventually, he stopped at a ladder that led up to the surface.

"Up you go." He gripped her waist and lifted her onto the second rung.

It wasn't a long climb. At the top was a round metal hatch. Marcus moved up behind her on the ladder and with one arm, opened the hatch and shoved it upward. It opened with a muted groan of metal.

Elle climbed out onto a flat part of roof made to look like rock that was edged with trees. She turned in a small circle, taking in her surroundings. The brilliant green of the trees caught her eyes. When she took a closer look, she realized the "trees" were actually disguised solar power arrays. Each of the leaves on the trees was a tiny photovoltaic cell used to generate power for the base.

Then she noticed what was set up over in one sheltered corner of the space.

A dark-blue picnic blanket was laid out, and sitting on top of it was a wicker basket.

He led her over to it.

She couldn't seem to close her mouth. "Where did you find a picnic basket?"

A small smile. "I can't give away all my secrets."

Once they were seated, he poured her a glass of something orange and fizzy. "Not alcoholic because we're on call."

She sipped the tart, sparkling juice. "It's lovely."

He reached into the basket. "I have some cheese and bread, and strawberries I had to barter with Hamish for from the hydroponic gardens." Marcus shook his head. "That old guy is protective of every berry and leaf. Oh, and some cured ham and olives."

Elle could do nothing more than just stare at the feast he'd set out on the blanket.

He shifted, bending one leg and resting his forearm on his knee. “I know it isn’t anything fancy, not what you’re used to from before—”

She reached over and grabbed his hand. “It’s perfect. No one’s ever taken me on a picnic, before or after the raptors came.”

Marcus pressed a piece of cheese to her lips. “I hope not. Otherwise I’d have to beat up him up.”

She smiled. “You’d win.”

They ate and stared at the sky. The sun turned the horizon a brilliant orange tinged with shades of pink.

“So beautiful,” she said. “Funny, considering how the world isn’t beautiful anymore.”

“There’s still beauty there. You just have to look a bit harder to find it.”

She turned her head and realized he was looking at her. God, the man was perfect.

“I was all about beauty before. I wanted the latest designer fashions, the perfect haircut—” she held up her hands and eyed her short, chipped nails “—and heaven forbid I didn’t have perfect nails. I had a weekly manicure appointment. What I saw in the mirror defined me, along with the parties I went to, the people I was seen with.” She shook her head. “You wouldn’t have given me second glance. I was so incredibly shallow.”

“Hey.” He tipped her chin up. “That might have been you once, but that’s not who you are now. I see a strong, confident woman who uses her smarts and determination to do the best she can to contribute around here. We can’t erase the past, and frankly, you shouldn't want to. It's brought you to this point. It helped make you who you are today."

She grabbed his other hand and he squeezed it.

He rubbed a thumb across her bottom lip. "We might still have regrets, but we learn from our mistakes and move forward." He let her go and picked up a strawberry.

Elle took a bite of the juicy berry, savoring the flavor. She thought she'd heard something buried in his voice. "Do you have regrets?"

He stared at his drink. "Yeah. Lots of them." He sighed. "Before the invasion, I led a UC Marine Force Recon team."

She'd heard of Force Recon. "Special Forces."

"Yeah. We specialized in deep reconnaissance, but we saw plenty of offensive action, too. Spent a lot of time in the Middle East."

He was silent so long she thought he wouldn't continue.

He glanced her way. His eyes had darkened. "If I tell you this story, you mightn't look at me the same."

"That could never happen," she answered emphatically.

With a nod, he stared at the last dying rays of the sun. "We were sent in to rescue hostages. They were a mix of innocent locals, women and children, and a few Western journalists. I made the call to wait, get more intel. Really, I was pissed to be on the mission. I wanted my team on the front line where I thought they could do the most good, save the most lives." He rubbed a hand over the back of his neck. "We were too late. We took down the kidnappers but the hostages were all dead. The women raped, the journalists had been executed, and the kids…fuck."

Her throat was tight. "You don't have to tell me."

"They'd tortured them. Cut off body parts and messed them up before they'd finally slit their throats."

Elle pressed a hand to her mouth. The horrible things he had to live with. And how many more terrible memories had been added since the raptors had turned Earth into their own private battleground. "You didn't kill those people, the enemy did."

"Yeah, but I didn't save them, either. But I get up every day and see if I can do better than I did before."

She slid closer. "You can't be a superhero all the time."

He tugged her under the curve of his arm. "Not according to my father. A Marine should be stronger, faster, smarter."

"What happened to him?"

"I assume he was killed in the first wave. I was over here on assignment and he was back home in California. He'd retired a few years back. I tried a few channels to try and contact him, but you know how it is."

She did. Blue Mountain Base had made contact with a few enclaves of humanity in North America, Asia and Europe, but transmissions were difficult and often blocked by raptor technology.

"I'd hoped he'd made his way inland to the Groom Lake base in Nevada...he's a tough old bastard. But when I did manage to get a transmission through no one there had seen or heard of him."

"I'm sorry." She pressed her face against his shoulder. "You were close?"

Marcus shrugged. "He was a Marine to the bone, tough as old leather, and he expected me to be tough, too. He wasn't my biological father, but he's the only one I've ever had. My mother got pregnant young and was kicked out by her family. She was waitressing, right up to when I was due, and Dad used to eat at the diner every day. He ended up taking her in, taking care of her, and fell head over heels for her. Don't know if she loved him back, but they seemed happy enough."

It appeared Marcus had inherited his need to protect those less fortunate from his father.

"My mother died when I was young so he was all I had. He did the best he could. He was proud as hell when I made the Recon teams."

An easy silence fell and Elle fiddled with the hem of Marcus' shirt. "You were lucky to have him. Nothing I did ever made my parents proud. I stopped trying after a while and became what they believed I was."

His arm tightened around her. "Babe."

She leaned into his strength. "I'm okay. My father never saw me. I didn't have the right anatomy, so I was just a pretty ornament. My mother loved me in her own way...but if I did anything remotely successful, she saw me as a threat, or competition. After a while I just excelled at being a party girl." She shook her head. "So pathetic."

"You aren't that girl anymore."

"I was engaged." He tensed and she hurried on. "Sort of. We never made it official. We just liked being seen together, the perfect, pretty couple. He was the golden son from a wealthy family and he excelled at partying more than I did." She sighed. "Aaron didn't see me either."

"You deserved better than they gave you."

"Maybe, but my parents didn't deserve to die the way they did." Her breath hitched. "Torn apart by raptors."

He hugged her close. "All we can do is move on. Make something of our future."

She leaned up and nipped his lips. "I like the sound of that."

"Hey, here's where you two are hiding."

Shaw's drawl had them drawing apart and Elle watched a scowl take over Marcus' face.

She looked up and saw Shaw, Cruz and Claudia dropping down on the blanket beside them.

"Ooh, strawberries." Claudia plucked up a berry and took a bite. "Old Man Hamish rarely lets anyone have any of these beauties."

"What are you guys doing here?" The tone of Marcus' voice left no one at a loss over his feelings about the intrusion.

Cruz winked at Elle. "Looking for food. I was

hoping for tamales, but while the chef here tries, they just don't taste like my father's did. And I wanted to see how you were doing, *amigo*. Make sure Ellie here was happy."

"And not in need of a rescue," Shaw said around a mouthful of cheese. "You aren't known for your flair with the ladies."

Elle smiled at them. Like it or not, Hell Squad was a family.

Marcus' scowl deepened and he tugged Elle closer into the curve of his arm. "Of course, she's happy."

"We can see that." Claudia smiled at Elle. "She's glowing."

Elle blinked. Claudia…smiling. It wasn't something Elle saw often.

Marcus sighed. "Where are Gabe and Zeke?"

"Beating each other up in the gym," Shaw said. "Couldn't pay me enough to spar with Gabe. The man is scary. I am so glad he's on our team."

"How's the translation coming along, Elle?" Cruz asked.

She released a long breath. "Slowly. I'm missing something, I'm just not sure what it is, yet."

"Something other than just difficulty with the language?" Marcus asked.

"I think so. The word combinations are strange. I've been wondering if there's some hidden encryption."

His hand massaged the back of her neck. "You'll get it. We knew they wouldn't make it easy for us."

"I know what they call themselves now. The Gizzida."

Shaw wrinkled his nose. "Ugly. Suits them."

Suddenly, a huge explosion ripped through the evening air. The ground beneath them trembled, and back toward the city, a huge, black mushroom-shaped cloud bloomed in the night sky.

"Shit. That's close." Marcus leaped to his feet.

The others jumped up, too. "Really close," Cruz added.

"Marcus, look." Elle pointed off to the north.

Red lights glowed in the sky, moving fast. A raptor ship.

"A ptero. Come on." He pulled her up.

All of them raced back inside, hurried down the ladder and hightailed it back to the main part of the base.

They ran into Zeke and Gabe.

"There you are." Zeke's face was grim.

"What do we know?" Marcus demanded.

They fell into step, striding toward the landing pads. Elle had to jog to keep up.

"A group of incoming survivors was heading this way. The raptors ambushed them. Holmes wants Hell Squad and Squad Nine out there."

"Okay. Suit up. I'll meet you all at the Hawk." Marcus turned to Elle.

"I'll get to the control room. Be careful out there." Fear was a sneaky invader, crawling through her belly.

Marcus yanked her up so her feet dangled off the ground. The kiss was hard, intense, and far too short. "I'll see you when we get back."

She watched him stride away, her heart beating triple time. Watching him head out into danger was so damn hard. Dragging in a deep breath, she raced toward the Comms Control Room.

Soon, she was seated at her station, headset on. Beside her, Arden, the comms officer for Squad Nine, was talking into her headset.

Elle turned her attention to her comp screen. The drones were up and giving back live feed. The two Hawks were converging on the attack site.

"One minute until you reach the site, Marcus."

"Roger that." His gravelly voice filled her ear.

She zoomed in on the images. Saw the raptors cutting down humans. Her stomach turned over but she kept the horror from her voice. She switched to the comp view—raptors marked in red, civilians in green. "It looks too hot for the Hawks to land. I suggest you rappel in."

"Got it. Any sign of that ptero?"

"It's not on screen. I'll keep an eye out. Be careful."

Shaw's voice cut across the line. "What about the rest of us, Ellie, girl? Or do you just care about Marcus' ugly mug now?"

"Off the line, Shaw," Marcus growled.

Elle fought back a smile. "Rescue those survivors and then *all* of you come home safely."

Shaw made kissing noises across the line and Elle heard Marcus growl again. Zeke was laughing.

The Hawk reached the explosion site.

Red dots flickered to life all over her screen. She

tapped it, taking readings. "Thirty raptors on the ground."

She heard the squad talking as they attached to lines and rappelled out of the Hawk.

"Fuck me," Zeke breathed.

"Raptors everywhere, Elle." Marcus' voice was grim. "They're picking off the survivors. We're going in."

Elle gripped the edge of her desk and listened as Hell Squad and Squad Nine engaged. There were yells, carbine fire, and the grunts and shouts of raptors. There were also screams and keening cries.

She closed her eyes, trying to find some sort of calm inside. Marcus would be all right. He and the squad were the best, they always came home.

"Get those survivors to the evac point," Marcus yelled. "Elle, we need a Hawk on the ground ASAP. We have civilians with severe injuries."

"It's a fucking mess." Ragged anger underscored Cruz's voice. "The raptors have been here a while torturing these people."

Oh, no. She tapped the screen. "The first Hawk is circling around. They'll be on ground in three minutes."

"Watch out!" Gabe's yell tore through the line.

"Dammit," Marcus bit out. There was more laser fire.

Elle watched as more red points poured out of a concealed location. *No. Where had they come from?* She heard the distinctive explosion of concussion grenades.

"Marcus! Another thirty raptors—"

"Hell! We see them."

She wanted to scream Marcus' name, make sure he was okay. She bit her lip, tasted blood in her mouth. Instead she stared at the blue dots of her team on the screen.

"I'm hit!" Zeke's voice.

"I'm coming," Gabe yelled.

"Give them cover fire," Marcus roared. "Claudia, get the last of those survivors over here!"

Elle patched a line through to the Hawk. "Finn, you need to get on the ground, now! It'll be a hot evac."

"On it, Elle," Finn's cool, calm voice came through the line. "We see them. Second Hawk is coming in right behind me."

She tapped a foot against the floor. Beside her, she heard Arden's urgent commands to Roth and his team.

A masculine yell ripped through the line and Elle jerked.

A blue dot blinked off the screen.

Her heart simply stopped. *No.* One of Hell Squad was…dead.

"Marcus?" She gripped her earpiece so hard it cut into her hand. "Marcus, do you copy?"

The only reply was the sound of laser fire and an inhuman wail that she knew was torn from a human throat.

"Marcus?" *Please, please answer me.*

Chapter Twelve

Marcus' jaw was clenched so tightly he thought it might break under the strain. As the side of the Hawk opened, he gestured to his silent and somber team to help the sobbing civilians off.

Only Gabe remained, sitting beside Zeke's body.

"Time to go, Gabe."

Gabe's hands curled into fists. "I will take down every single raptor on the entire fucking planet."

"And I'll help you. For now, let's get Zeke to Doc. You know she'll do right by him."

Gabe gave a rough nod and for a second, Marcus caught a glimpse of the man's gray eyes. They looked like thunderclouds boiling and brewing before a storm. He was always intense, but now something frightening was alive in his eyes.

Marcus didn't let himself think or feel as he picked up Zeke's body. Not yet.

Doc Emerson stood near the Hawk, an iono-stretcher hovering behind her.

And beside her stood Elle, her hands clamped together in front of her and her face etched with grief.

A flood of conflicting emotions rushed through Marcus. And leading them was guilt.

He'd been enjoying himself with Elle, and he'd taken his eye off the ball. Now, one of his team had paid the price and the rest of them were bleeding from the wound.

As the sobbing survivors were checked over by Doc Emerson's staff, he stared at a shell-shocked little boy sitting on a chair, covered in blood. His ears had been cut off.

For a second, Marcus flashed back to other children left dying in pools of their own blood. Another time he'd been too concerned with his own goddamned wants and needs to do what had to be done. To be one step ahead of the bad guys.

He set Zeke's body down on the stretcher.

"I'm so sorry, Marcus," Emerson said. But her gaze strayed over Marcus' shoulder to Gabe, standing like a silent sentinel on the other side of the stretcher.

"Take care of him." The words sounded torn from Gabe.

"I will." The doctor looked like she wanted to reach out to the grieving man. But after a second, she nodded. "And we'll do what we can to help the survivors."

Marcus ground his teeth together. "The raptors had them for a while. Torturing them."

"Like I said, we'll do what we can. But they'll need time for the emotional wounds to heal. You got them out of there, that's what counts."

But at what cost? So many of them had terrible injuries and Marcus knew better than most that sometimes the emotional scars never healed.

And now Zeke was dead.

"Marcus."

Elle's voice was a balm but at the same time made his guilt spike. He wanted to pull her close and bury his face in her hair. Just hold on and forget for a second.

But as he watched the stretcher move away, with the body of a good man going cold on it and the man's broken brother walking beside it, he couldn't bring himself to touch Elle.

Zeke would never laugh, never spar with Gabe, never hold a woman again.

Instead, Marcus held up a black crystal. "They left this at the attack site for us to find. We need to know what's on it. *Now.*"

Elle took it and nodded. "Okay." She reached her other hand for him.

Marcus side-stepped her. "I need to check on Zeke…and Gabe. I'll come to the lab soon." He walked away and forced himself not to look back.

It took him almost an hour to prize Gabe away from his brother's side. Emerson was taking great care with Zeke's body, but seeing the once-vibrant man and badass warrior with all his armor stripped away…seeing his body so still and white on the damn bunk in the infirmary left Marcus feeling a sick mixture of despair and fury.

He needed to find that comms hub. And blow the fucking raptors to hell.

He needed to stay focused on his mission and not on organizing picnics and kissing sweet, full lips.

Marcus slammed into the comp lab.

Elle's head shot up. She sat hunched over her comp console. The screen in front of her was filled with raptor symbols and she held a stylus poised above her tablet.

The sick look on her face made his gut clench. "What?"

"Marcus, I don't think—"

"Tell me what you found, Elle."

Her gaze darted away and she took a deep breath. "They left a message on the crystal."

He strode over and looked over her shoulder. She held a spread palm over the tablet but then, reluctantly, she inched it away.

They died in payment for your continued, futile attacks on us. Their blood is on your hands.

The more you fight back, the more we will retaliate. More will die.

Marcus breathed through his nose, fighting back the vicious emotions storming through him. He wanted to stride down to the cells below and tear their raptor prisoner apart with his bare hands.

Instead, he settled for slamming a fist into the desk. The table jolted, rocking the comp screen.

Elle watched him, biting her bottom lip. "It's not your fault, Marcus."

"I didn't have my head in the game. I was too twisted up thinking about—" He had enough sense to cut off his words, but he saw her flinch. He knew he should say something to make it better. And he knew he was being an ass, but he just didn't have it in him right now to be anything else. "Find the comms hub."

She nodded. "I won't stop until I do."

There were other things he wanted to say and do, but all he could see in his head was Zeke's blank face and that little boy covered in blood. "I…have to go."

Elle's lips pressed into a flat line. "Okay. I'll get to work."

He turned and walked away.

"Marcus?"

He paused but didn't look back. He was afraid he might collapse at her feet, tug her into his arms and never let go.

"You're not alone," she said quietly. "Remember that."

As he slammed out of the lab, he'd never felt more alone in his life.

***

Marcus jabbed his fist into the boxing bag hanging from the gym ceiling. As it swung, he followed with a powerful kick that rattled the chain holding the bag, then he slammed a sequence of unforgiving punches into the battered leather.

Sweat dripped into his eyes and soaked his T-shirt. He'd been in here since he'd dragged himself out of his bunk that morning, and after he murdered the bag, he was going to lift some weights.

It had been two days since Zeke had died.

Two days since a good man's body had gone cold.

He hadn't heard from Elle, so he assumed she

didn't have a location yet. He hadn't seen her, hadn't seen anyone. He'd either been in the gym or sitting up on the roof in the darkness.

"What the hell do you think you're doing?"

Cruz's voice made Marcus jerk around. His friend stood there in black cargo trousers and a black T-shirt. Menace radiated off him.

"Working out."

"You haven't spoken to the team. You haven't seen Gabe. You haven't turned up for training. I didn't think moping was your style, Marcus."

Marcus felt a muscle in his jaw tick. "If that's it, you can leave. Or I'll kick your ass instead of this bag."

Cruz shook his head. "The team's doing okay, by the way. Well, about as okay as we can be right now. I'm worried about Gabe, he's silent at the best of times, but now he won't talk at all. He keeps disappearing and won't tell me where he's been. But worst of all is what you've done to Elle. I thought you cared about her, wanted to protect her."

Marcus stilled. "I haven't done anything to Elle."

Cruz made a rude noise. "You told her to find the comms hub, Marcus. No matter what. What did you think Ellie was gonna do, *amigo*?" The man shook his head. "She's fucking working herself to the bone, you idiot. She hasn't slept, hasn't eaten."

Marcus' heart kicked his ribs. "What?"

"She'll kill herself trying to decode that raptor gibberish. You guys are perfect for each other. You're here blaming yourself, she's blaming herself.

A pair of idiots."

"Cruz—"

The other man chopped his hand through the air. "Save it—"

Marcus grabbed Cruz's shoulders and shook him. "Is Elle all right?"

"No. She's exhausted and looks sick."

Shit. Marcus released him and scraped a hand through his hair.

"Look, Marcus, blame the damn raptors for Zeke, not yourself. Then make Elle get some sleep."

Marcus was already headed for the door. He jogged through the tunnels. He had to get to her.

When he stepped into the lab, she was in her usual position, hunched over the keyboard. He frowned. What the hell was Cruz talking about? She looked fine.

"Elle."

She flinched and glanced over her shoulder. His gut took a hit. Her face was deathly pale and her eyes were sunken and underscored with black circles. She didn't just look tired, she looked dead on her feet.

"I'm really close, Marcus. I made a few mistakes and got tangled up for a bit because the symbols seem to move around, but I'm back on track." She lifted a hand to brush her hair off her face. Her hand shook. "I've narrowed it down to a certain radius. The hub's in the suburbs somewhere south of the city, near the airport. A few more hours and I hope to crack it."

"When did you last eat?"

Her gaze skittered away, back to the screen. "I'm not hungry."

He stepped closer. "That's not what I asked."

"I don't remember. Our…the picnic, I think."

Marcus swore and watched her curl in on herself.

"I'm not going to hurt you," he bit out.

"I know," she whispered.

"Come on. You need to eat."

A little life sparked in her eyes. "No. I have to find that hub."

"Now. Or I'll carry you."

"I don't like you much when you get bossy."

"I don't care."

"Look—" she stood and took one step.

She collapsed.

Marcus lunged forward and caught her. "Dammit! Elle?"

"I…don't feel very well." Her eyelids fluttered closed and she fainted.

Marcus swung out of the lab and headed straight for the infirmary. She'd be all right. She *had* to be.

"Exhaustion," Emerson pronounced, checking Elle's eyes with a tiny light.

"I'm fine," Elle protested from where she lay on a bunk.

"She needs rest and something to eat. Something packed with calories."

Elle tried to get up. "I said—"

"Be quiet." He scooped her back into his arms. "I'll take care of her."

They were silent as he strode toward her quarters. At her door, she pressed her palm to the lock and the door released.

Her room was almost identical to his, but of course Elle had added small touches that made hers seem more homely. A small carving of a bird sat on a shelf along with a small collection of old-fashioned books. A blanket that was a swirl of blues and green sat folded on the end of her bunk. And on the bedside table was a framed picture of Hell Squad with Cruz, Zeke and Shaw holding Elle up sideways. She was grinning and glancing up at Marcus where he stood beside them, his arms crossed.

They were his family now and he'd let them down. Again.

He had to make things right. Starting with taking are of Elle.

"Shower," he said.

Her eyes flashed. "I'm fine now. You can go."

"Elle, get in the shower, or I'll strip you myself and put you in there."

She pressed her lips together, then stomped into her bathroom. Once he heard the water running, he hurried next door to ask the teenage girl he'd spoken to last time to grab some food from the dining room.

Once Elle reappeared, wrapped in a fluffy towel, he directed her to the bed and sat behind her. He picked up the brush he'd found in the bathroom. It felt far too small for his big hand but he was determined to take care of her. His carelessness had brought her to this.

When the hell would he quit screwing up and hurting people?

He started stroking the brush through her damp hair.

“I’m sorry about Zeke,” she said softly.

Marcus paused, then resumed stroking. “He was a good soldier, a good man.”

“Is Gabe okay?”

“No. But he’s tough. He’ll pull through.” Marcus gripped her hair. “I’m sorry I haven’t been to see you.”

“I don’t want to talk about it. I’m tired.”

His jaw tightened but he let it go for now. After a few more strokes, her head fell forward and she made a small moan. Partway through, her neighbor knocked on the door with a tray of food.

Marcus thanked the teenager before closing the door in her curious face.

He forced Elle to eat some bread, soup and fruit. He also managed to get half a cup of tea into her. Then he went back to the rhythmic strokes of brushing her hair. Damned if he didn’t find it almost hypnotic and her hair was so soft, like silk. His mind was quiet for the first time in days.

Elle’s breathing slowed and her shoulders drooped. She slowly relaxed back against him and dropped into sleep like a child.

Marcus stayed there a long time, not wanting to disturb her. He just watched her sleep, the delicate rise and fall of her chest. Eventually, he settled back on the bed, pulling her with him. He thought she was still asleep but he felt her muscles tense.

"Shit, I didn't mean to wake you," he said.

"I'm feeling much better." Her words were stiff.

He dragged in a breath. "I'm sorry I ignored you."

She shrugged. "It's okay, you—"

"No, baby. It isn't. I was messed up. I was angry and grieving, and I took part of it out on you."

"You shut me out," she said, her tone blank.

"I know. I shut everyone out."

"When you're with someone, you're supposed to lean on them. Share how you feel. In the good times and the bad."

"Never been good at that." He stroked a thumb over her lips. "Never wanted to be."

"Unless this is just sex. Just fuck—"

He shook her. "No."

She watched him for a moment. "You hurt me."

Those softly spoken words speared into him and hurt worse than any bullet or laser burn. He tightened his arms around her. "I know. I'm sorry." He shifted, rolling until she was tucked beneath him. "Whatever you want me to do to make it up to you, I will."

Her eyes were closed and he hated that. Hated being shut out.

"Look at me, Elle."

Her eyelids lifted and those luminous blue eyes seemed to see all the way inside him.

"I can't promise I won't hurt you again. I'm a man and not one who's easy with his feelings. But I want to protect you, I don't want to hurt you. I'll try my best not to do it again."

Her lips trembled and her face softened. "Okay."

"We okay?"

She nodded.

Then he moved his hips until he knew she'd feel the hard bulge of his cock against her thigh. "Let me make it up to you.

Her tongue darted out to lick her lips and heat flared to life in her eyes. "You'll have to work pretty hard."

A laugh escaped him, everything inside of him easing. "Well, baby, you're in luck. Marines have excellent stamina."

She helped him tear open his pants. As he stood to shuck off his boots and trousers, she cupped his cock, teasing him.

With a groan, he pushed her back on the bed and covered her with his body. Keeping his gaze locked with hers, he pushed inside her, slowly. Inch by tortuous inch. She moaned, her hands clutching at his back.

Damn, she was so hot and tight. But he was going to go slow this time if it killed him. Which it just might. "Now I'll say sorry the best way I know."

Chapter Thirteen

Elle woke in the darkness, disoriented. Had she fallen asleep at the computer again?

Then she felt the big, hard body surrounding her and heard quiet breathing by her ear.

Marcus. She relaxed into him. He was so warm.

God, the last two days had been horrible. The way he'd backed away from her and shut her out. It had dented her heart a little. She turned onto her side and she could just make out his face in the dim light.

Even in sleep he didn't look relaxed or softer. He was hard and tough and his scar made it so he'd always look a little scary.

But not to her. Never to her. The way he'd taken care of her this evening…she shivered. It had her wanting more. Much, much more.

He was her anchor. Her sanctuary. A center in the storm.

Center.

The word triggered something in her head.

She blinked. God, that was it!

She slid out of the bed. She needed a tablet and the raptor map symbols. Damn, all her stuff was in the lab. And she was naked. She nabbed one of

Marcus' T-shirts off the floor and yanked it on.

It was huge on her, hanging almost to her knees, and it smelled like him. She paused for a moment, lifting the fabric to her nose and breathing him in. Then she spotted his tablet lying on the table.

She nabbed it. She felt a tiny twinge of guilt as she did it, but it took her about two minutes to break his password. She'd picked up some useful tips from Noah.

She curled up in the armchair, then paused. There was a picture of her on the background. A candid shot of her smiling, one she'd never noticed him taking. She pulled in a breath. "Oh, Marcus."

Shaking herself, she linked to her directory on the network and pulled up the raptor map. This had to be it! She tapped out notes, muttering to herself as she erased some things and added others.

"Elle."

Marcus' deep voice made her look up.

He stood a meter away, watching her, and all thoughts of the map evaporated in a puff of visceral lust. He was naked. Every heavily-muscled inch of him on display.

"What are you doing?" He came closer and cupped her shoulder, massaging the joint.

She blinked. "Doing?"

"Yes, you're sitting here in the dark muttering to yourself when you should be sleeping. From now on, if you have a nightmare or can't sleep, you wake me. I'll make sure you can get to sleep."

She felt heat rush into her cheeks, picturing

exactly what he'd do to help her. "I didn't have a nightmare." Marcus' arms seemed enough to ward off the dark dreams. "I think I've worked out the raptor map!"

"Come back to bed. You need more rest."

She glanced down at the tablet. "I think...wait, that's the final bit." She grinned as she tapped the screen. She was right! Now it made sense why she couldn't narrow down the location past a general area. "A modulating encryption."

"What?"

"They're using a hidden modulating encryption. It changes, mixes everything on the map around. The hub's somewhere in the old airport, Marcus. You have to be close to it, within a certain radius, for it to give the final part of the encryption and show the exact location. But now we know where to go to find it."

He smiled. "See, you just needed some sleep and rest to work it out."

Elle felt heat in her cheeks. "I just needed you."

He knelt and moved between her legs. "Do you need me to say I'm sorry again?"

She shook her head. "I know Zeke's death was a terrible blow..."

"Yeah. But it didn't give me the right to hurt you." Marcus fingered the hem of her...*his* shirt. His fingers brushed her skin, making her tremble.

"We're okay," she murmured. "Just don't do it again."

He tugged the shirt up an inch. "You look good in this."

"Marcus." She grabbed his hand. "We can find the comms hub."

He nodded. "I never doubted you'd work it out."

His simple, honest confidence in her made her glow. Then she realized the full implications of the modulating encryption. Her stomach cramped. Oh, God, Marcus was not going to be happy.

She fiddled with the tablet. Best just to get it out there and get past the fallout as soon as possible.

"Marcus, I'm the only one who can read the final encryption. I need to get close to the hub." She swallowed and lifted her gaze. "I need to be on the mission to destroy the comms hub."

He froze. "No."

She pressed a hand atop his, where it rested on her thigh. "I have to. There's no other way."

He shot to his feet, oblivious to the fact he was naked. "I told you, no more missions for you. And after this last fuck-up..."

She stood and walked to him. She pressed her hand to his back and the muscles tensed so tight they felt like they'd snap. "That just makes finding this hub and destroying it more important. Now we have to do it for Zeke."

Marcus' hands squeezed into fists. "Dammit!"

She slid around in front of him and curled her hands over his fists. "I'll be with you. And Hell Squad will be watching our backs. We can do this, Marcus. In and out."

He dropped his head until his forehead hit hers. "You don't get hurt. Not *one* hair on your head."

She swallowed. "Okay."

"Not one hair, Elle. I mean it. Or you will get that spanking."

She felt her shoulders relax. He was going to let her go. She lightened her tone. "Promises, promises."

He gripped the neck of her T-shirt. "I want this back now." With a flick of his wrist, he tore the shirt down the middle.

Elle gasped. "You have to stop doing that."

When he picked her up and dropped her on the bed, all she could do was hold on and enjoy the ride.

***

Marcus stood at the edge of the trees, hands shoved in his pockets. He stared down at the simple marker set on the ground under a large gum tree.

"He liked sitting out here. Watching the stars." Gabe's murmured comment was toneless, his gaze turned up to the night sky.

Marcus had spent the day planning the hub mission and then this time with the team. He wanted to believe Gabe was doing okay, but the man had lost his twin, his best friend. He was going to need a hell of a lot of time for that open wound to scab over.

"He was good man." *Sorry I let you down, Zeke. I promise to watch over Gabe for you.* "And a hell of a soldier."

The rest of Hell Squad and Elle stood behind them. Grief pulsed off them all.

"And the best brother I could have asked for," Gabe added quietly.

Elle sniffled and Marcus moved back toward her. She stepped forward, squeezed his hand and moved up beside Gabe. "We're all here for you, Gabriel. Whatever you need, you just have to ask."

Gabe, always the loner, brushed his knuckles across her cheek.

"Zeke had a hell of a smile," Claudia said. "It was no wonder the ladies loved him."

"And he had a mean right hook." Shaw slung an arm over Claudia's shoulders. And for once, she let him.

Cruz stepped closer. "I envied his focus, the way he threw himself into every battle without blinking. He always told me we were fighting for those who weren't as strong as us and that was a worthy cause." Cruz smiled. "Zeke told me he liked being a hero."

"And a hero he was," Elle murmured.

"To Zeke," Marcus said.

They stood there for a while, lost in their memories, just the wind rustling the leaves in the trees.

"Now, it's time to go and make those bastards pay for taking Zeke from us," Marcus said. "We don't go in half-cocked, looking for revenge." He caught Gabe's gaze. "We go in and follow the plan. Destroying the hub will hurt them way more than killing a few alien soldiers."

He looked at each one of them, assessing. He needed to know they had their heads screwed on right.

"Ready to go to hell?"

"Hell, yeah," they all yelled. "The devil needs an ass-kicking!"

"All right. Let's get suited up and to the quadcopter."

Marcus kept himself focused on the mission as they prepared and boarded the Hawk. His usual battle readiness descended as they took off, his heart beating in a steady rhythm.

It wasn't until the quadcopter's skids touched dirt, that thoughts about taking Elle into hell…again…hit him. *Stay focused on the mission, Steele.*

He leaped out and shouted directions to his team. He watched Cruz help Elle down. Marcus had found her some armor that fit her smaller frame better. He knew she also had her thermo pistol and a mini-gladius knife he'd slipped into her boot.

Marcus touched the strap of the black, carbon fiber backpack he wore. Nestled inside, about the size of a soccer ball, was the bomb they'd use to destroy the hub.

The quadcopter lifted off and swung west above the trees and disappeared into the night. They were on their own now. They wouldn't even have any comms support except for Elle. To limit the risk of the raptors picking up the signal, there'd be no comms back to base.

Elle fiddled with the mini-comp screen attached to her wrist. "So, why are we here? So far from the airport?"

"We have to drive in," Marcus said.

"Too many raptor aerial patrols over that part of the city." Cruz looked east, to where the once-busy international airport lay. "They know we're trying to decode their map. They'll be ready for us and it's gonna be hot. That's why we're going in under the cover of dark."

Marcus looked and saw red lights in the sky, zipping back and forth. His jaw tightened. Yeah, the bastards knew they were coming.

Dammit, he wished that Elle wasn't with them.

But then he looked at her and saw the set look on her face. There was that quiet determination. If she was feeling nervous, he couldn't see it.

"All right, Hell Squad, let's get this show on the road." As Marcus turned, he saw Gabe. The man stood a little apart, cradling his carbine. His face was set, too, with a dangerous, ruthless edge that would either keep him alive or get him killed.

Marcus sure as hell wasn't losing anyone else from his team.

Holmes had wanted to put Gabe on leave but Marcus had fought it. He knew Gabe needed this. He moved up beside the man.

"Jackson, I need to know you have your head screwed on straight."

Gabe's face remained impassive. "Don't have a death wish, if that's what you're asking."

"Partly. You're a part of this squad and we take

care of our own."

Gabe nodded. "I'll do my job, Marcus."

"For Zeke."

Something painful flashed across Gabe's face, then was gone. "For Zeke."

Marcus moved back toward Elle and saw her looking around the few ramshackle sheds scattered around the site.

"Are we walking?" she asked.

"Nope."

They were at what had once been a secret military testing facility. He strode over to the largest shed. He shifted a panel of corrugated iron and uncovered a shiny keypad. He typed in the code and a large, camouflaged door slid open.

Elle studied it, wide-eyed. "What is this place?"

"We'll talk once we're inside." Marcus waved them in.

No one relaxed their guard. They moved down the wide, concrete-lined tunnel that descended to a lower level.

Slim lights on the wall clicked on automatically. After they'd traveled down several dozen meters, the tunnel opened up into a small underground parking garage.

Five armored personnel carriers were parked against the wall. All of them were black and looked like large SUVs on steroids, each with an autocannon mounted on top.

"APCs," Elle said. "I've never seen any like this."

"Z6-Hunters." Marcus patted the armor-plated hood of the nearest vehicle. "These were only in the experimental stage when the invasion happened. This installation was a testing facility. These babies had to go into service a little ahead of schedule. They have experimental armor and weaponry and top-of-the-line illusion systems. We'll take the first two. Cruz? You, Gabe and Claudia in one. Shaw and Elle, you're with me." The other three moved off and Marcus nodded to the autocannon.

Shaw shot him a wide grin. "Thought you'd never ask."

"Try *not* to shoot anything. We want to keep a low profile."

Elle tugged at the door handle and opened the passenger door.

Marcus closed it. "In the back."

Her face turned mutinous. "Enough with the orders. You can order them around—" she jerked a thumb at the team "—but not me."

Marcus was speechless. He heard one of the others snicker.

She straightened. "Now. How about you try *explaining* why you want me to sit in the back."

He blinked. "It's safer. The windscreen is reinforced, but a raptor mortar could still get through. I want you in the back."

"See? Was that so hard?" She climbed into the backseat.

As he shut the door, he fought back a smile. She might look sweet, but there was a sharp little edge to Elle. And he liked it.

In the driver's seat, Marcus started the engine.

The heads-up display flared to life, glowing blue-green. He touched a screen on the dash and it filled with a feed to Cruz's Hunter.

"No headlights," Marcus said to Cruz. "Only use night vision and ensure the illusion system is activated."

Elle leaned forward through the small gap to the backseat. "We should keep off the old highways." She was looking at the comp screen on her wrist. "I've worked out the safest route to the airport using smaller roads. I'll shoot it through to the APC computers."

Marcus nodded. That was his girl. "Got that, Cruz?"

"Got it." Cruz's voice came through clearly, like he was seated beside them. "Map's coming up now."

Marcus looked back. "Shaw? You set?" He could just make out the sniper's lower body where he sat in the elevated cannon seat.

"Hell, yeah. Ready to kick some alien butt!"

"Roll out." Marcus put the Hunter in gear and headed up the ramp.

He followed the route Elle had mapped out. They passed damaged houses and stores, overgrown parks, apartment buildings. Some were in ruins, others were fully intact, like the owners were going to come home any minute.

But no one was coming home.

They passed the burned-out shell of a school. A tattered banner still tied between two trees proclaimed "Enrolments Now Open."

"It's so sad," Elle said quietly.

Marcus glanced in the rearview mirror and saw her staring out the window.

"So much death. Nothing will ever be the same."

"Don't be sad, Ellie-girl," Shaw called down. "Still plenty of life left in us yet." The sniper leaned down to look at her and waggled his eyebrows. "I'm sure the boss man's been showing you that."

She reached back and smacked Shaw's leg. "I was being deep and emotional, you idiot."

"You were moping."

With a smile on her face, she looked forward and her gaze caught Marcus' in the mirror. Her smile turned soft, a private one just for him.

Yeah, they were surrounded by lots of death and destruction, but when she looked at him like that, he'd never felt more alive.

They continued on, the roads widening as they approached the airport. Twice, they had to stop while raptor patrols passed overhead. The Hunters' illusion systems helped hide them, but it didn't make them invisible.

Soon, the now-overgrown, open space of the runways appeared. And in the distance, the glimmer of moonlight on water. Sydney's airport had been the country's busiest, with its major runways jutting out into Botany Bay.

But it was the giant alien spaceship that captured all their attention. It sat, crouched like some enormous scaled beast, ready to pounce. No, that wasn't quite right. Marcus thought it looked more like it should be slicing through the water with its sinuous body and fin-like wings.

He still remembered seeing it that first night of the invasion, appearing over Sydney and causing widespread panic. It had hovered for over an hour, and reports from all major cities around the world had shared similar stories. Then the smaller ptero ships had been launched and the world as they'd known it had ended.

"We need to find somewhere to hide the Hunters." Elle's voice broke into his thoughts. "I think in the suburb adjacent to the Domestic Terminal. There used to be a bunch of hotels and some industrial buildings that serviced the airport." She tapped at her mini-comp. "Then the best way to the hub zone is through the old train tunnels." She tapped again. "Okay, I've found an old warehouse where we can leave them. From there, it's a straight shot to the old Mascot station."

Marcus drove slowly through the debris-strewn remains of the once-vibrant area. Once, there would have been a steady flow of planes arriving and departing every day. Now, he saw broken aircraft strewn against the fence by the side of the road, like ruined carcasses caught in a net.

His usual crystal-clear calm that allowed him to function at peak performance wouldn't come to him. Instead, Elle's presence made him feel something he rarely felt on a mission. Fear.

"Where are the raptors?" Claudia asked across the comms.

Marcus stared at the street ahead of him and wondered the same thing. He felt like a small animal being led into a trap.

Soon, they pulled up to the warehouse Elle had found. They parked the Hunters inside the cavernous space and hid them between the forklifts and trucks.

"All right." Marcus checked his weapon and pressed the button that had his combat helmet sliding into place. "Let's get to the train station."

It was a short walk. The team kept alert and Marcus watched for any sign the raptors were watching them. Before long, he saw the single-story station building, with its now cracked blue sign proclaiming "AirportLink."

Inside, the once-modern station was coated in a layer of grime and dirt, and filled with leaves, trash and other debris. They pushed through the turnstiles and descended the stairs to the darkened platforms below.

The squad flicked on their tactical flashlights attached to their carbines. On the platforms, it almost looked as though the alien apocalypse had never happened. Except that a train sat on the track halfway into the station, and it looked like someone had once sheltered on the opposite platform. Marcus moved his light around. A pile of blankets and a few other scavenged goods lay in a heap on the tiled floor.

"It's spooky down here," Elle whispered, the dim glow of her comp screen casting a pale light on her face.

"Which way?" he asked.

She pointed. "That way."

Into where the train lines ran into the darkened

tunnel mouth.

Then she froze. "I saw something."

Marcus tensed, felt his team sharpen around him. "Where?"

She shook her head, peering at the opposite platform. "Maybe just a shadow."

Then Marcus saw it too.

Something moving in the darkness.

Chapter Fourteen

Marcus shone his light in a steady sweep across the platform.

Elle started to think that perhaps her nerves had gotten the better of her and she'd imagined the movement. Until she saw them.

A couple of humans huddled together near what might have been a vending machine. She gasped. *Kids*. They looked to be about fifteen, if they were lucky.

"Hey, we aren't here to hurt you," Marcus called out. "You can come out."

The teenagers didn't move.

Elle shook her head. "You're too intimidating, Marcus." She leaped down onto the tracks.

"Elle!"

Too late. She was already scrambling up onto the other platform.

Behind her, Marcus' deep voice rasped, "Stay here, Hell—Squad Six."

"Because we're too intimidating?" Shaw's voice was ripe with amusement.

As Marcus growled, she hid her own smile, and a second later he was moving up beside her with a lithe leap.

She approached the boy and girl slowly. “How long have you been down here?”

The boy kept a tight arm around the girl. Both were painfully thin. “Not sure. We’ve lost track of time. Months, I’d guess.” His wary gaze swung from her to Marcus. “Who are you guys?”

“We’re from Blue Mountain Base,” Marcus said.

The girl looked at him with wide eyes and pressed closer to the boy’s side.

Elle held out a hand. “My name’s Elle Milton and this is Marcus Steele.”

The boy hesitated for a second. “I’m Leo and this is—”

“Clare,” the girl whispered.

“Nice to meet you. Have you heard about Blue Mountain Base?”

They shook their heads.

“It’s a base west of the city. Full of survivors. We have food, clothes, medical help, books, even schools. And these tough guys here—” she pointed at Marcus, then the rest of Hell Squad “—they protect us. They go out and fight the aliens.”

Leo’s eyes grew so large they overtook his face. “You fight them?”

“Yeah,” Marcus said gruffly.

Clare pulled away from Leo and grabbed Elle’s hand. “You have food? And books?”

Elle stifled a smile. Trust the girl to be more worried about books than medical help. “Yes. And you can both come.”

Clare’s lips trembled. “Really?”

“Really. But I need you to be brave a bit longer.”

She hated doing this. "We have a mission to complete first. Then we'll come back and get you."

Leo's eyes turned dull. "Right. Sure."

Elle gripped his hand, too. "We *will*. Our vehicles are hidden aboveground. That's how we'll escape after we blow up the raptor communications hub."

Leo considered her words, then nodded. "Okay. But you should know, down there—" he nodded toward the tunnels "—there are so many aliens. Tons and tons. I've snuck down there, seen them." He shivered. "Heard them."

"Thank you, but we know." She squeezed his hand again. "Our mission is very important. And we'll be back. My team here, they're called Hell Squad. There's no team tougher and no team better at taking down raptors."

Leo pulled Clare to his side again. "Good luck. We'll be here."

"Stay hidden," Elle said. "We *will* come for you. I swear."

Marcus was watching her with bemused eyes. As they joined the rest of the team, he tipped her chin up with an index finger. "You were good with them."

"They're tired, hungry and afraid. I remember what that feels like. They just needed some honesty and compassion."

"We'll come back for them," he promised.

And she knew Marcus always kept his promises.

"All right, Hell Squad." Marcus eyed his team. "How about an evening stroll through alien-infested tunnels?"

"Oh, yeah," Shaw responded.

"I'm ready," Gabe said.

"Bring it," Claudia added, lifting her carbine.

Cruz gave a nod.

Elle dragged in a breath and nodded as well.

Marcus leaped back onto the tracks. "Let's go start some fireworks."

But as the dark tunnel swallowed them and the team flicked their night-vision lenses over their right eyes, Elle felt the dense black push in around her.

She clutched her thermo pistol and tried to relax. The night-vision lens felt foreign, and the green glow it gave everything was eerie. And there were still too many shadows for her liking.

She felt like the tunnel was closing in around her.

Suck it up, Elle. She lifted her chin and kept moving. They had a mission and she was going to get the team there.

Marcus gripped her arm and made the "okay" sign with his fingers. She nodded. His presence calmed her jittery nerves. She consulted the map on her wrist and led them deeper into the tunnel.

Her steps made the slightest scuffing noise on the ground. The rest of the squad moved with a ghost-like silence she envied. Claudia and Cruz were ahead, carbines up, staring down their sights. Marcus was with her in the center and Gabe and Shaw were bringing up the rear.

They should be in the map encryption range

soon. Then, the final part of the encryption would fall and she'd be able to pinpoint the exact location of the hub. She eyed the backpack Marcus was carrying. Crazy to think it held a bomb and that such a small thing could cause so much destruction.

Something flickered to her right. Elle slowed her steps and turned her head.

Nothing.

Giving her head a shake, she started moving again.

Another movement. Deep in the shadows. Maybe it was more survivors? Elle stared harder. But all she saw was darkness.

Great. Now she was seeing things.

"Anything?" Marcus murmured through their earpieces.

"Nothing," Cruz replied. "Quieter than a bachelor at a bridal shop."

Shaw snorted.

They moved on but again, a minute later, Elle saw something else move in the shadows. Something low to the ground. Too small to be a raptor, surely?

She stopped and kept staring.

"Elle?"

"There's something moving over there." She nodded her head.

Like a well-oiled machine, the team moved as one, weapons up.

"I don't see anything," Cruz said.

Elle bit her lip. Maybe she'd imagined it.

Claudia would have a field day.

"If Elle said she saw something, she saw something." Marcus was staring down the sight of his own carbine. "Gabe?"

Gabe shifted, his head cocked. "I can hear something breathing."

Elle blinked. There was no way he could hear anything that soft.

Gabe moved forward, his big body flowing like a panther on the hunt.

Elle's heart was pounding. Suddenly, a quiet growl filled the tunnel.

Gabe stiffened but kept moving.

Please, be a dog. Please, be a regular, normal dog. Elle bit her lip.

Three canids leaped out of the shadows, snarling.

Gabe fired, but the canids were on him in seconds, knocking him to the ground.

"Stay here." Marcus brushed past her. The others were running forward as well.

She realized they couldn't fire with the alien dogs so close to Gabe. Marcus ripped his gladius from its sheath and plunged it into the closest creature. Claudia did the same with the second animal.

The third canid leaped off Gabe, its claws red with blood, and rushed at Cruz.

Cruz dropped his carbine and stayed still, arms raised.

Elle took a stumbling step forward. What was he doing?

The canid hit him. Cruz grabbed the creature around the neck, using its motion to spin and with a firm twist, broke the canid's neck.

With a yelp, the dead canid dropped to the ground.

"Fucking hell." Gabe pushed to his feet, shaking his head. Blood soaked his shoulder.

"How bad?" Marcus asked.

Gabe snatched up his weapon, double-checking it. "Not bad. Got a claw in under my armor. It'll stop bleeding soon."

Claudia grabbed a med-patch from her first-aid kit. "Here."

Gabe nodded his thanks and slid the patch under his armor.

Scratching noises from behind Elle reached her ears. Heart kicking her ribs, she slowly turned around.

Her mouth dropped open and she stumbled back toward the team. "Marcus." She kept her voice low, calm.

"What?"

She bumped into him and pointed.

"What the hell?" he murmured. "Hell Squad, weapons hot."

Dozens of alien...creatures were slinking toward them from the depths of the tunnel. Some on the ground and others scurrying along the roof and walls.

Elle lifted her pistol. Her hand was steady. Mostly.

They looked like canids, but their bellies glowed

with a sickly red color. Like their insides were filled with something hot and nasty.

“Shit, what are these things?” Claudia said.

“Some kind of mutant canids,” Marcus murmured.

Suddenly, the creatures swarmed, racing forward with snarls and growls.

The sound of carbines firing echoed thunderously in the confines of the tunnel. A huge, glowing canid landed in front of Elle, its jaws open, slavering as it stalked closer to her.

She raised her pistol. When the creature’s muscles bunched, she didn’t hesitate to fire.

Elle kept her finger on the trigger. The thermo bullets ripped open the belly of the animal. Red ooze splattered everywhere and the canid fell on her. She slammed into the ground, the air knocked out of her, the dead mutant canid on top of her legs.

The scent of something burning filled her nose. She kicked at the alien and looked down.

Oh, God. The red goo was sizzling, eating through the metal train tracks beneath them and through her cargo trousers.

She kicked, trying to get the animal off her.

Hands gripped her under her arms and yanked her back. She craned her head and saw Marcus holding her.

“It burns.”

His face was grim. He grabbed the water bottle off his belt and upended it over the bottom of her trousers.

It hissed as it hit the acidic fluid, and the

burning stopped.

"Must be like what they put in their weapons." Marcus yanked her up. "Come on—"

An enormous, glowing canid slammed into Marcus' back, its claws sinking into his armor and the backpack containing the bomb.

As they crashed to the ground, Elle almost fell backward. She looked around frantically for help. But the rest of the team were all still firing at the continuing mass of mutant canids swarming them.

She spotted Marcus' carbine on the ground. She snatched it up and jammed it against the canid's thick neck and fired.

The weapon's kick was more than she expected and she stumbled back.

The canid jerked, then slumped forward. With a massive heave, Marcus threw the body off him.

"Thanks," he said. "Not just a pretty face, are you?"

"No, I'm not."

He tugged her close to his side and took the carbine back. He quickly felt the backpack. "The bomb's still there."

"And it didn't blow up," she added.

The team was still firing and the canids were still coming. The walls of the tunnel looked like they were painted in red acid.

"There are more headed this way!" Cruz shouted.

"We're barely making a fucking dent," Shaw called as he wielded two weapons at once, his carbine, and a deadly-looking pistol.

Cruz grabbed a grenade off his belt and glanced at Marcus. "Destroy that hub and look after her. She's the best thing that's ever happened to you, *amigo*. She makes you smile and soothes those very rough edges of yours." He yanked the pin off and strode into the oncoming canid swarm.

Elle felt Marcus tense, and panic welled in her. They *couldn't* lose Cruz. She struggled in Marcus' grip. "No!"

But Marcus held her back.

"Ah, fuck no." Shaw cursed in a low, steady stream.

Cruz pulled his arm back and tossed the grenade deeper into the mass of red canids. It exploded with a fierce bang. Many went down, but the surviving creatures all turned and began loping toward Cruz.

He fired his carbine.

The squad fired too.

But Elle could already see there were too many alien animals. They closed in on Cruz.

"We have to go," Marcus said, voice grim. "Now!" He forced Elle ahead of him.

Elle choked on a sob. Her last glimpse of Cruz was of him being surrounded by the mutant canids.

Chapter Fifteen

Cruz

Cruz waited for the aliens to rip into him.

He closed his eyes. He felt strangely empty. He'd been running on empty for far too long. Most days, he couldn't remember why he was fighting anymore. And since Zeke had died…

Suddenly the tunnel filled with high-pitched yips and yowls.

His eyes snapped open.

Deadly black bolts whistled through the air, hitting the lead canids.

His gut hardened at the sight. *Familiar* black bolts.

The first bolt exploded on impact. There was a hissing noise as the bolt sprayed a mist into the air and across the alien beasts. Their cries turned to pained howls. Some dropped to the ground, writhing. The rest, as one giant mass, whirled and ran back into the darkness.

"What the hell?" Cruz felt the fine spray coat him, too. It smelled like…green trees?

Sudden shouts from his teammates echoed in the tunnel as they ran back toward him.

"Cruz?" Marcus raced forward. "You okay?"

The substance clung to him, giving off a faint glow, and he smelled like a fucking forest. It didn't seem to burn or hurt him in any way. "I'm fine."

"You are a crazy son of a bitch," Shaw yelled. "What the hell did you think you were doing?"

"Saving your life," Cruz snarled back.

"Well, someone sure as hell saved yours."

"Yeah." Cruz turned, eying the blackness where the bolts had come from.

A figured emerged from the shadows, walking toward them. Tall, slim, dressed in black cargo trousers and a hooded black top. His savior had twin Shockwave laser pistols holstered on narrow hips and held a modern tactical crossbow at their side.

Cruz couldn't look away. He felt like every cell in his body was paying attention.

"It's *you*," Cruz said. "You helped us before. At the library."

The figure nodded, then pushed the hood back.

Cruz barely contained his jerk of surprise. *A woman.*

She had a long fall of black hair pulled back in a tight ponytail. Her face was typical of the melting pot that was Australia's races but from the fine features and caramel-brown skin, Cruz guessed she had some Indian heritage. Her eyes were a unique pale green.

"I suggest you move fast." The woman toed the body of dead canid. "These things hunt in large packs. They'll bring reinforcements."

"What are they?" This from Gabe, who was crouched beside one of the creatures, eyeing the red-stained belly.

"Another alien abomination. I call them hellions."

"You've encountered them before?" Marcus asked.

"Yes."

Cruz stepped closer. "Who are you?"

"Santha. Santha Kade."

Santha. "My name's Cruz Ramos. You live here?"

"In the city."

He tugged at his damp collar. "What was the spray?"

Her lips moved in a small smile. "Sometimes the simplest things work the best. It's a mixture of several items but the main ingredient is cedar oil."

Gabe straightened. "We used to use cedar mulch back home to keep snakes out of the yard."

The woman nodded. "It contains something that's toxic to reptiles. Alien reptiles included. But it only seems to work on the canids and hellions."

"We'd be much obliged if you'd share that recipe with us," Marcus said.

The woman inclined her head. "I'd be happy to."

Cruz drank her in. Something about her pulled at him...he wanted to know everything. "We're from Blue Mountain Base, west of—"

"I know where it is."

"There are lots of survivors there. Food, hot water occasionally. Come with us."

She stared back at him for a moment, then shook her head. "No. I'm staying." She glanced at Marcus. "You're planning to destroy their communications?"

"Yes," Marcus answered.

"I haven't been able to pinpoint its exact location. I take it you know where their hub is, then?"

Elle raised her arm and the mini-comp. "We have a map. We're still working on the final encryption, but we're close."

Santha nodded. "And you're headed in the right direction. I'll wish you luck then." She turned. "Like I said, you should move fast."

"Thank you," Marcus said. "If you ever need anything, ask for Marcus Steele. Or Cruz." He nodded at the team. "Move out, Hell Squad."

"Wait." Cruz grabbed Santha's slim shoulder. Under the fabric, he felt toned muscle.

She paused and raised a brow.

There was pure, undiluted confidence in her eyes. This was a woman, and a warrior, who knew exactly what she was good at. But there was something else there too. A dangerous weariness he recognized all too well. Something he saw reflected in the mirror every day.

Cruz glanced at Marcus. "We can't leave her."

"Looks like she'd doing okay for herself." Marcus nudged Elle along.

"Please, come with us," Cruz tried again.

"I'm staying and fighting for my home." For a second, Santha looked like she wanted to say something else.

"You could fight with us." He smiled at her. Maybe some charm might help. "We have resources, training—"

Her lips twitched. "You can put the sexy grin away, soldier. I'm not that easy. I work better alone…but thank you."

Cruz ground his teeth together. He barely knew her, but some part of him didn't want to let her go.

Green eyes clung to him for one more second. "Stay safe."

She disappeared into the darkness.

Cruz just stood there, staring after her.

"Cruz, we need to move. Mission, remember?"

Cruz muttered under his breath. "Yeah."

He dragged his attention off his mysterious savior and back onto the mission.

***

Marcus watched a stationary train appear out of the green-tinged gloom ahead.

Around him, the squad was wired and wary.

As they passed the train, he saw Elle frowning at what looked like rust on the metal. But he noted the red-brown stains were smeared all over the windows too. It was no rust.

Then her brow scrunched and he knew she understood what those stains were. He saw her swallow a few times.

Marcus touched a hand to the nape of her neck. She looked up, her face set but steady. It broke his heart a little to see her learning to hold her own in the field, to see horrible things and deal with them. But he was damned proud of her as well.

They reached a junction, two tunnels spearing off in opposite directions.

"Which way?" he asked.

Elle tapped her mini-comp. The encryption still hadn't broken but they had to be getting close. "Ah, right, I think."

"Think or know?"

She stiffened her spine. "Right is all I've got for now. As soon as this encryption falls, I can give you more."

Somewhere behind them, Claudia snickered. Marcus hid his smile. Yep, he was really starting to like those moments when Elle bared her teeth.

They moved down the tunnel, this one narrower than the earlier one with only one track. Suddenly Elle's mini-comp beeped and the screen flared.

"Encryption's down." She swiped the screen, tapping at the map. "We've got it! We've got the hub's exact location."

"About damn time," Shaw muttered.

Marcus ignored him. "Where?"

"About another fifty meters down this tunnel, there looks to be a service door into what was the Domestic Terminal's train station." Elle looked up. "From there, we have to head up into the terminal. To the food court. The hub's in there. Feeding off what was once a small reactor used to power the terminal."

"Okay, Hell Squad, let's finish this." Then he

could get Elle out of here.

They continued on and stopped at a metal door marked "Maintenance."

"Cruz, get it open."

Cruz pulled something off his belt and got to work.

"You can pick locks?" Elle whispered.

"Man of many talents, *querida*."

Yeah, Cruz had a lot of talents Marcus didn't ask too much about. He had a dark past he didn't like to share. Marcus watched his friend work and pondered the interest Cruz had for their attractive savior.

Marcus was damn happy about it. For months, he'd slowly watched his usually-happy, carefree friend turn harder and more disenchanted with the world.

Marcus looked at Elle. His own personal ray of sunshine. Sensing his scrutiny, she looked up and smiled. A tiny flicker of calm washed over him.

Cruz stepped back and opened the door.

Marcus gestured with his hand and the team moved inside the station. Seconds later, they crept up some stairs and past the turnstiles.

There was another wide tunnel lined with tiles and covered with advertisements for comps, banks, supersonic business travel to the world's financial capitals, an island holiday on the Great Barrier Reef.

At the end of the tunnel, they found a pair of now-still escalators and walked up.

The first level was baggage claim. Some belts lay

empty and others were still loaded with suitcases. Some other bags were strewn about, torn open, their contents spilling onto the tile floor.

Elle pointed up again.

This time it was check-in. Rows of empty check-in machines stood silent, their comp screens blank.

The squad spread out. Elle pointed them on toward the security checkpoint under the large Departures sign.

Gabe went first, moving toward the inoperative security machine that Marcus knew had been introduced a few decades back. The high-tech systems could simultaneously check for weapons, traces of explosives, and drugs, and also did a biological sweep for illness and signs of elevated nervousness. The technological advancement had cut security incidents on planes dramatically.

Gabe ducked through the arch.

Lights flared and an alarm screeched through the cavernous terminal.

Shit. Marcus pulled Elle down behind a row of chairs. The rest of the team took cover and waited.

Nothing.

Dammit. This was either a big decoy and the team was going to find nothing.

Or the raptors were welcoming them in before they sprung a dirty, big trap.

It didn't matter. Whatever happened, they had to destroy that hub.

After a tense wait, no aliens appeared. Marcus directed the team onward and they skirted the security machine.

"Left," Elle whispered.

On one side were large glass windows showing empty gates or planes waiting for passengers who'd never come. The other side was a row of shops. A bookstore with a small section of paper books and rows of comps that would have offered quick downloads of the latest digital bestsellers. A ladies' clothing store that had been looted long ago. A jewelry store with rows of once-expensive watches in the window, now worth nothing.

"There's the food court," Elle said.

The team halted and Marcus studied the open area ahead. Rows of tables and chairs filled the center of the space. Fast-food restaurants that once offered everything from burgers to sushi lined the walls.

"Too damn quiet," Gabe murmured.

Yeah. Marcus scanned the area but didn't see anything moving.

Elle tapped furiously on her screen. "On the other side of the food court, there's an entrance to a maintenance room that houses the nuclear reactor that powered part of the terminal."

"And the hub?" Marcus asked.

She looked up. "The raptor hub is directly below the reactor. Looks like there is a staircase down to it."

Marcus hated when a mission was too fucking easy. It always meant a big pile of shit was going to rain down. And raptor shit stank really, really badly.

He eyed the maintenance door across the

expanse of the food court. He wished again, for the thousandth time, that he didn't have to take Elle in there.

"Let's move."

They moved through the tables, every member swiveling around as they went, carbines aimed, waiting for raptors to pour out of some unnoticed hiding place.

Cruz smashed the lock on the maintenance door and pushed it open. Marcus went first and the team followed.

The maintenance area was large. Metal pipes ran across the ceiling, sending water and power to different parts of the terminal.

A big, boxy reactor sat in the middle of the space, humming quietly. Power filled the air, making the hair on Marcus' arms stand up.

The raptors' part-organic, scale-covered cables ran from the reactor, disappearing toward the back of the room.

"The stairs are that way," Elle whispered.

He nodded and moved forward.

As they crossed the space, the only sound was the dull thud of their boots on the floor.

Too damned quiet. Marcus had barely finished the thought when he saw a flash of movement.

Clunk.

Something landed and rolled toward them.

Smoke exploded in a thick gray cloud.

"Smoke grenade!" someone yelled.

Marcus ducked. Where was Elle? He tried to peer through the smoke but it was worse than soup. He heard throaty growls.

The raptors were here.

Heart pumping in his chest harder than it ever had, he crawled across the concrete floor. Where the hell was she? He bumped into something. Something warm.

"Marcus?" A shaky whisper.

Relief almost took him to the ground. He curled his body around her. "I got you, baby."

"I can't see." Her hands gripped his armor.

"It'll clear in a few seconds. Then we fight. Keep your head down."

He felt her fingers travel up his chest, brush his jaw. "Be careful."

"Will do. You be ready to tell us where to go next."

He felt rather than saw her nod. But soon he could see her pale face in the murk. He knelt and swung his weapon up. As soon as he started firing at the vague moving shadows on the other side of the room, his team opened fire.

Shit, there were a lot of raptors. Then he heard a low, raspy laugh. God, he hated when they did that.

The ground vibrated. Marcus kept firing, his pulse tripping. A huge raptor, twice the size of the others lumbered into view. He carried some sort of weapon Marcus had never seen. It was huge.

"Marcus? You see him?" Cruz's voice came through the dissipating smoke.

"Never seen one like him before." That rasping deep laugh echoed around them again. This time it made Marcus' muscles tense.

"*Fiiiire.*"

Shit. It had spoken. In *English*. Shock froze Marcus for a second. Then, the super-raptor lifted his weapon and flames exploded outward.

"Flamethrower," Marcus yelled, diving for cover. He reached out, trying to find Elle, and only fining air.

A wave of fire rushed over them, scorching hot. *Hell on Earth.*

Chapter Sixteen

Flames exploded everywhere.

Elle swallowed, and kept her head down. Her throat was bone dry from the hot air surrounding her.

She heard that terrifying laugh, felt the ground shaking with each heavy footstep. *Oh, God.* Suddenly, hard fingers clamped down on her arm.

"Move. Now."

Marcus. She jumped to her feet and followed him. When she glanced over her shoulder, her stomach dropped away.

An enormous man…dinosaur…creature stood a few meters away, swinging a huge weapon that was spewing lethal fire. She saw he was aiming at Cruz and the others who were pinned down on the other side of the room.

"Elle, focus."

She snapped her head forward and narrowly avoided tripping over a dead raptor.

Marcus pushed her into a narrow space behind some workbenches. He fired again, trying to help the others.

She smelled a horrid smell and realized part of her hair sticking out from under her helmet was burning. She slapped at it.

Under the barrage of fire, the large raptor finally pitched forward, the flames cutting off. Elle drew the tiniest breath. Then she saw another swarm of armed raptors racing in.

Marcus touched a finger to his ear. “Cruz, keep them busy. We’ll make a run for the hub and plant the bomb.”

“Roger that,” Cruz responded. “Keep your head down and keep Ellie safe.”

Marcus’ gaze found her face and her heart skipped a beat.

“Count on it.” His tone was deep gravel.

She followed him to the stairs. These ones curled down in a spiral into blackness. She checked her comp screen again, but the image blurred. Terror turned all the raptor symbols to gibberish.

The nearby gunshots rang in her ears. God, her entire body was shaking.

“Hold it together.” He grabbed her hand, his gloved fingers secure on hers, and tugged her down the stairs. “You can do this.”

At the bottom was a solid-metal door. Marcus shot at the blinking control panel and the door opened with a hiss. They stepped inside and she saw nothing but impenetrable darkness.

The door closed behind them and cut off the last of the light.

“Shit.” Marcus yanked at the door, then kicked it. “It’s locked.”

Okay, not necessarily a bad thing. It would stop the raptors getting in. She turned back to the thick darkness. But what if something was already hiding in here?

In an instant, she was back in that closet in her parents' home, bombs exploding outside, her mother sobbing, her father yelling, a raptor grunting in the dark.

"I can't do this." She stepped away from Marcus. She'd been wrong to push him to have her on the team.

Marcus clicked on the light mounted on his gun. It cut a bright shaft through the blackness. "Elle—"

She shook her head wildly. "I can't do this. I'm just a useless party girl." Who'd done nothing while her parents were killed. "I can't do this. I was stupid to come, to put you all at risk."

Marcus gripped her arms, gave her a none-too-gentle shake. "You aren't that woman anymore."

"What if you're wrong—?"

"Have you ever known me to be wrong?"

She blinked and focused on his serious face. God, she loved those tough features. He was real. Solid. While she felt like nothing.

"I see quiet strength." His big hands framed her face. "I see a quick mind. I see an amazing woman. A beautiful woman who makes my gut tight every time she smiles, or laughs, or just looks my way. I see the woman I'm in love with."

She stilled. All the raging emotion in her emptied out in a rush. She stared into his eyes. New emotions rushed in to fill the hollow, empty space. Desire, wonder, something else she was afraid to name.

His thumb brushed over her lips. "You gonna say something?"

She shook her head. She couldn't speak if her life depended on it.

"I've seen you, Elle, from that first day I found you covered in raptor blood."

She couldn't believe it. That this man felt something more for her. "Marcus…"

She wasn't sure if she moved first or if he did, but in the next breath, they were kissing.

It wasn't gentle or pretty. It was hard, rough and it had desire roaring through her. God, she'd never felt anything like what Marcus made her feel. His tongue swept into her mouth and the force of the kiss bent her head back.

This was real. Hot, real and something to hold on to in the dark. He swept an arm around her and tugged her into his chest. She slid her hands into his hair and pulled him closer. She never wanted it to stop. She wanted the wild explosion and the earth moving to go on and on.

Until she realized the explosion was a grenade going off upstairs and the building was shaking.

Marcus pressed his forehead to hers, his breathing heavy. "Let's get this done and when we get back to base…"

He left the promise open and she shivered. She knew exactly what he had planned. "Then let's get this finished as fast as we can."

His white teeth flashed in the darkness. "Nothing like the right motivation. Come on, the guys won't be able to hold them off forever."

She touched her comp screen and the dull glow seemed bright in the dark. The map came into perfect focus. "We need to go straight ahead. The hub should be located on the back wall."

Marcus led the way, turning his head, listening for any sounds.

They reached the back wall.

It was empty. Just a blank sheet of bricks.

Elle's heartbeat was a heavy pounding in her ears. "It's supposed to be here. The map says it's right *here*."

"Dammit." Marcus looked to the ceiling. "I knew this was too easy."

"Marcus?"

He slammed his boot into an empty cardboard box on the floor and sent it skidding. "It's a set-up. I knew they were toying with us."

Elle shook her head. They couldn't fail now. They'd come too far.

Marcus turned to face her. "We need to get out."

"No. It *has* to be here." She tapped at the screen, searching the map again. "Maybe I read it wrong? Or made a mistake? That has to be it."

He gripped her hand. "You don't make mistakes."

"I used to." She felt the burn of threatening tears. "I used to make them all the time."

He touched her face. Big, tough hands that were so gentle. "But you don't now."

Damn him, she didn't want to cry. "Oh, Marcus—"

The boom of a weapon reverberated through the

small room. Elle watched as Marcus flew back and hit the wall.

No! She saw the blood, smelled it.

Marcus' blood.

Elle dropped to the floor and scrambled closer to him. His carbine had fallen to the ground, the light spearing into the darkness.

She fumbled at her belt, reaching for the thermo pistol. She tried to pull it out, but it was stuck and her damned hand was shaking so hard.

A sound.

The scrape of a foot.

She swiveled. And saw the raptor.

He looked like a man in the cloak of shadowy darkness. But as he moved into the halo of light from Marcus' dropped weapon, she saw the thick, scaly skin. His sharp teeth glistened in his elongated face. His eyes glowed red, and in them there was intelligence, sharp and cunning.

He was so damned big. She managed to yank her pistol out and heard the raptor snort. She had to protect Marcus. She crawled in front of him. *Please, please let him be alive.*

The raptor stepped closer. He lifted some small device and pressed a button. Behind her, light shimmered, and she turned her head to look.

A hologram camouflage. It disappeared and she saw the hub, exactly where is was supposed to be, lights blinking and flashing. Feeding communication to the entire alien horde.

Anger churned. *So close*. She felt something sticky on the floor. Knew it was Marcus' blood.

She lifted the pistol. It shook wildly.

The raptor cocked his ugly head with something resembling a grin on his face. He moved forward, not seeing her as a threat.

Too many people had written her off. She hadn't been smart enough for her father, pretty enough for her mother, charming enough for her fiancé. She'd never even believed in herself.

Until now. Until the last few months working as part of a team, giving it everything she had, helping others.

Now Marcus' life was in her hands.

Her hands stilled. She fired.

The raptor stumbled, his body jerking. She kept pumping the thermo bullets into him. They glowed gold in the shadows.

He dropped to his knees and made a keening sound that made her wince.

Then her weapon clicked. She looked at it. *Oh, no.*

The raptor laughed. A low, rasping sound that made her blood freeze. He lifted his gun.

Elle felt a touch at her hand. She glanced down, saw Marcus' blood-covered fingers press his large gladius knife into her hand. It was black. Big and rugged. A warrior's knife.

"Kill. Him." Marcus' words were a near-silent whisper.

She grabbed the knife and launched herself forward. The raptor stiffened, she saw his demon eyes widen. She hit him, burying the blade into the softer flesh at his throat.

He made a terrible gurgling sound and the rank stench of his breath hit her. His gun clattered to the floor. As he fell backward, Elle pushed herself off him, rubbing her hands on her thighs to rid herself the horrible sensation of scales pressed to her skin.

Then she scrambled back to Marcus.

God, no. She saw the shredded, torn mess of his middle. His armor had taken the brunt of the force but an ugly bone-like projectile stuck out of him and beneath him a large pool of blood was forming. It was bad.

She ripped a small first-aid kit from her belt and pressed a wad of gauze to his wound. He moaned. She looked up and saw green eyes watching her.

"I'm so sorry, Marcus."

"Nothing to be…sorry for. Saved…us."

"I should have done something." She grabbed his hand with her free one and lifted it to her chest. Pressed it to her heart. "I'm sorry I was such a coward. I should have—"

"You took him down. Brave."

He had such belief in her. "I never thought, in a million years, that you'd be interested in a woman like me, let alone love me." She felt a tear slide down her cheek. "I love you so much. I wish I'd told you months ago how I felt."

He managed to lift his hand to her cheek, brushed his knuckles down her cheek. "I was a coward. Told myself…didn't want to sully you with my rough hands—"

She gripped his hand, pushing her cheek into his

hot palm. "You idiot. You're such a good, solid, fearless man."

"Elle. You need to plant the bomb."

She swallowed the sharp lump in her throat. "Okay. I'll do it for you."

She helped him take the backpack off. Every wince and groan made her want to cry. She unzipped the bag and pulled the spherical bomb out. It wasn't that big but she knew it would bring the entire terminal down. She helped him press the code in and it awakened, lights flashing.

Elle carried it over to the hub. Strong magnets activated and it slammed into the side of the hub and started humming.

She hurried back to Marcus. Sliding down beside him, she tangled her fingers with his. She hated seeing him slumped against the wall, lines of pain bracketing his mouth.

"You have to go now," he said.

"No." The whisper was ripped from her. The thought of leaving him left her nauseous. "I'm staying."

"Dammit, Elle. I've fought…so you'd be safe. Go. Live." He lifted a hand, trying to reach her but it was clear his senses were failing.

Deep grief tore through her. It couldn't end like this. "I want to live *with* you, not without you." She gripped his hand.

"I wish, baby." His fingers clenched on hers, released. "Kiss me. One last time. Then go find Cruz and the others."

She leaned forward, heedless of the tears that

streamed down her cheeks. She touched her lips to his. This was where she was supposed to be, in this man's arms.

He pulled back. "Now go."

"No."

He growled. "I want—"

A loud beep came from the bomb. They both glanced at it. Marcus was frowning. "Timer can't be…up yet. What the hell is it doing?"

"I don't know," she said.

"Go!"

She moved in close beside him. "I can't leave you."

"Elle—" Urgency in his voice.

A bright-blue flash broke out of the bomb, filling the room with light as bright as day. Pain seared Elle's eyes, digging into her head. Her hand clenched on Marcus' and she heard him shouting.

Then the light contracted and Elle felt her consciousness slipping away.

She pitched forward, her face hitting the ground, and darkness slammed into her.

Chapter Seventeen

Lights shone in Elle's eyes, but her vision was blurry, fuzzy.

Even the noises reaching her ears sounded muffled, as though they were coming through water.

"Fuck!"

She thought it was Cruz's voice, but she wasn't sure.

A handsome face leaned over her. But she couldn't move, couldn't talk.

Where is Marcus? She needed Marcus.

People talking. Then raised voices. "We're losing him!"

"Gotta move."

The snarls and guttural shouts of raptors.

Elle felt her body being jostled around. But everything felt so heavy, every muscle in her body made of lead. *Marcus. Marcus!* His name echoed in her head.

Her eyelids drooped closed and she couldn't pry them open again.

***

"Ellie? Wake up, *querida*."

The coaxing voice brought Elle out of the fog. She glanced at the pipes running overhead along the ceiling. She shifted and realized she was lying in a bed.

In the infirmary.

Back at the base.

She sat up, fighting the sheet covering her. "Marcus?" Where was he? She glanced wildly past Cruz and saw the other beds all lined up in a row.

They were empty, sheets pulled neatly over them.

Elle gripped Cruz's shirt. "No!" He couldn't be gone, not just as she was getting her chance.

"Hey, calm down." Cruz set his hands on her shoulders. "Your head took quite a knock."

"Marcus?"

She saw Cruz's lean face harden.

"Oh, no." She shook her head, felt a tear on her cheek. "He's dead." She'd failed him, too.

"Hey." Cruz rubbed a thumb over the teardrop. "No crying. You know Marcus is too tough to die."

Something unfurled inside her. Something bright. "He's alive?"

"Yeah. Lucky bastard nearly didn't make it." Cruz tapped her nose. "We found you both unconscious. The bomb had proximity security to stop anyone tampering with it once the countdown started. Knocks everyone in range out cold. Marcus had just about bled out, we lost him there once or twice—"

Elle made a choking noise.

Cruz hurried on. “But I pumped him full of nano-meds. Those little buggers kept him together long enough for us to get out, grab those kids you found, and get far enough away before the bomb went ka-boom.”

Elle pushed Cruz away and swung her legs over the edge of the bed. She was only dressed in a large T-shirt, but it hit her at the knees and covered enough. “Leo and Clare are okay?”

Cruz smiled. “Gorging themselves on anything and everything in the dining room. Well, when Clare pulls her nose out of whatever book she’s found.”

Elle stood, and gripped the bed as her knees wobbled. She needed Marcus. She had to see for herself that he was okay. “Where is he?”

“You need rest, *querida*.”

“ *Where*?”

Cruz let out a gusty sigh, but he was smiling. “You two are perfect for each other. Stubborn to the bone.” Cruz helped her take a few steps, hovering at her elbow. “He refused to stay in bed too, and watching you sleeping was making him crazy. I think he was worried you wouldn’t wake up.”

“Cruz,” she snapped at him.

“He’s on the roof. Quadrant Two.”

Elle hobbled through the tunnels, shocked that she felt so weak. But the burning need to see Marcus pushed her on.

She reached the ladder to the surface. It took her a while to climb it, since she had to stop for a few breaks to catch her breath. The door at the top was open and finally she stepped out into the crisp, pre-dawn air.

Out on the eastern horizon, murky light was just starting to tint the day.

And she saw the silhouette of the man who'd captured her heart.

She broke into a run.

Soldier that he was, he heard her, even though she hadn't made a sound. He spun.

"You shouldn't be out of bed." He closed the gap between them and pulled her in close.

She pressed a cheek to his chest. "Same to you."

"I couldn't..." His gravelly voice cracked. "I hated seeing you so still."

"I'm not the one who got hit by a raptor gun blast. You're okay?" She slid her hands up over his shoulders. Then she pushed back, her hands going to the hem of his T-shirt, tugging it up.

Oh. The reality of him always stole her breath. Probably would when they were both old and gray as well. She splayed her fingers over the hard ridges of his stomach. There wasn't an ounce of fat on him. And not even a scar from his wound. He was so...hard and strong. Warm and alive.

She moved her fingers, caressing that impossibly hard stomach. He hissed in a breath.

To affect this strong man with such a slight touch...

"I'm a hundred percent. Emerson put me back together." His hands cupped Elle's cheeks. "Elle." He leaned down and took her mouth.

Sensation washed over her. The cool air on her

bare legs, the heat of his hard exploration of her mouth, and the burn of desire searing her belly.

With a groan, he grabbed her, lifting her like she weighed nothing. She wrapped her legs around his waist.

"I love you, Marcus."

"God, sweetheart, I love you too." His arms tightened around her. "You're mine now. I'm not letting you go."

"Good, because I'm going to hold on to you too. Whatever happens, whatever we come up against." She stared at his tough, scarred face. A face so precious to her.

She knew for all the horrors that had happened, this she would never change. The chance to become someone she liked, the chance to have this man's love.

And she knew with him by her side, she could meet whatever challenges came their way. Together.

***

Marcus breathed in Elle's unique floral scent.

Alive. She was alive, warm and soft in his arms. *Thank God.* He never wanted to see her lying still and pale like that in a bunk again.

"I have a lot of plans for you," he murmured against her lips. "And they involve not getting out of my bunk…for a really long time."

"Yes." She nipped at his bottom lip, her smile a little reckless and a lot happy. Then it slipped away. "It seems so wrong to feel so incandescently happy when the world around us has fallen apart."

He cupped her bottom, pulling her in close. "We have nothing to feel bad about. The bomb we planted, it crippled the raptor communication in the area. You did it, Elle."

" *We* did it. For Zeke."

The thought of Zeke hit Marcus under his ribs. "Yeah, for Zeke." *Rest in peace, buddy.*

"It won't keep the raptors down for long, will it?"

"No, we know they're working to regroup, but for now, they're running in circles, confused. It's a good start and we'll keep fighting. For our chance to live."

She ran a palm over his shoulder. "It won't be easy."

He cupped her cheek. "No, it won't."

"You and Hell Squad will keep going out there, fighting, risking your lives." Her voice hitched.

"Hey." He forced her gaze to meet his. "I have something to come home to now, someone to live for."

She nodded.

"It's always darkest before dawn, sweetheart." He pressed his forehead to hers. "But even the longest night always ends."

She smiled. "I never thought Marcus Steele would say something so poetic."

"Don't tell the guys." He smiled back, stroking her cheek. "For now, we just have to find whatever light we can, hold on to it, and use it to guide us until the sun comes up."

"I think I'll just hold on to you instead. You've been my anchor ever since this all happened."

"Elle…" A light in the sky caught his eye. He looked up above her head, and surprise rocked him. "Shit, look, sweetheart. How's that for a guiding light?"

He set her on her feet, spinning her so her back was pressed against him. Damn, he was so happy she was his. He wrapped his arms around her as she arched her neck.

There, burning across the darkness, was a comet. A brilliant, white-blue flash in the black sky.

She snuggled into him. "Beautiful. They were considered omens in the past."

"Well, we both know it's just a hunk of space rock." He rested his chin on the top of her head. "But I'd like to think it is an omen—one of better things to come."

Elle spun and grabbed Marcus' hand. "I can think of some better things we can do right now."

He let her tug him back toward the door. "Sweetheart, I think the dawn is breaking for both of us."

I hope you enjoyed Elle and Marcus' story!
Hell Squad continues with CRUZ, the story of Hell Squad's sexy second-in-command and the mysterious Santha Kade. Read on for a preview of the first chapter.

Don't miss out! For updates about new releases, action romance info, free books, and other fun stuff, sign up for my VIP mailing list and get your free copy of the Phoenix Adventures novella, *On a Cyborg Planet.*

Visit here to get started:
www.annahackettbooks.com

FREE DOWNLOAD

JOIN THE ACTION-PACKED ADVENTURE!

Formats: Kindle, ePub, PDF

Read the first chapter of Cruz

Crouched in the shadows on the roof of a half-destroyed bank, Santha Kade looked through her high-tech binoculars and watched the alien invaders patrolling the streets below.

A year ago, these dinosaur-like raptors had decimated the Earth. Their huge ships had appeared in the skies...then they'd launched a vicious, unforgiving attack. Now they had bases in all of what was left of the planet's major cities.

Here in Sydney, the once-shining capital of the United Coalition, they'd ruthlessly razed the city. They'd left skyscrapers in tatters, the Harbor Bridge a shattered ruin...and humanity broken, afraid and on the run.

Santha's hands curled around her binocs. So many had died. Millions of lives...gone. Some survivors remained hidden in what had once been their homes, but they were slowly moving on or being weeded out by the raptor patrols.

She reached for her weapon. Her hand closed on her Titan tactical crossbow—the metal was cool under her fingers and the self-loading mechanism was filled with her own homemade bolts—and she felt herself grow calm, steady. Some gave up, some ran...and others chose to fight back.

She zoomed in with the binocs and studied the face of the lead raptor. Thick, gray, scaly skin covered his elongated face and his eyes were blood red. The aliens were all big—over six and a half feet—and carried a lot of muscle. They wore a kind of metallic armor on the bottom half of their bodies, and huge boots. Their top half was all tough skin, crisscrossed with what looked like leather for holding their claw-like blades, or for the snipers, their bone-like projectiles.

Looking at them made Santha's throat close in a choking rush. Why the hell had they come here? Why, with no warning, had they decimated the human race? Destroyed friends and families. Killed beloved sisters. She lowered the binocs and gripped her thigh. Her fingers dug into her skin through her black cargo pants.

It didn't matter. She didn't care. Whatever their reasons, she was going to make them pay.

Focused, she lifted the binoculars again.

The raptor at the back of the patrol came into view and a muscle ticked in Santha's jaw.

This one was the leader for this area. Santha was sure of it. She'd been spying on them for months, taking notes, marking down their installations, picking off small raptor patrols when she could.

She wouldn't ever be able to find the raptor that had beaten her sister to death, but she could sure as hell take down the one who'd given the order. Who'd brought these aliens here and ordered them to kill.

This raptor was a little taller than the rest, skin smoother and a darker shade of gray. Santha had nicknamed this alien, *the commander*. The commander had an air of authority and looked at everything like it was his—or her, who knew what gender they actually were?—domain to rule.

Not for long, asshole. Santha lowered her binoculars and took a deep breath. She wanted to leap off the building and shoot the commander through the goddamned head. Another deep breath. But not today. She needed more intel first, and she wanted to take out the leader and their main base in the city.

She caught a movement in the sky out of the corner of her eye. As she stared at the bright, blue expanse, she didn't see anything but fluffy white clouds.

She kept staring. *There.* A blur of something winked for a second.

Santha knew what it was. A Hawk quadcopter, with its illusion system up, flying in from the west.

Other humans were fighting back, too. From a secret base west of the city.

She watched where she guessed the camouflaged Hawk was flying and wondered if Hell Squad was on there. If *he* was on there.

She only had a little contact with the few survivors still hiding in the city. Most had left for the country or for Blue Mountain Base—the underground military base that had become a haven for survivors. But everyone had heard of Hell Squad. A group of soldiers so deadly, they mowed through the aliens as easily as taking an afternoon stroll.

Normally, she would have written that sort of reputation off as exaggeration, but she'd seen them in action. She'd even helped them a couple of times.

And she watched them…a lot.

Especially the sexy soldier with the dark, liquid eyes, sensual grin, and an accent that made her insides flutter.

Cruz. His name was Cruz Ramos.

She'd met him several weeks ago, when she'd helped them fight off aliens so the squad could get in to destroy a key raptor communications hub.

Hell Squad had blown the damn thing sky high. And for a month, the raptors had scrambled around with limited communications. It had made Santha's job a hell of a lot easier. She'd spent days out picking off lone raptor patrols who couldn't call for backup, and blowing up their facilities.

But they'd recently repaired the damage.

Santha shivered and shifted her binocs to where she'd last seen the Hawk's illusion. She caught a glimpse of gray steel as the copter dropped lower to land. She told herself to stop watching and focus on the raptors instead. After a quick—and futile—mental debate, she lifted her binocs again.

Zooming in gave her a perfect view of the now-visible Hawk in an empty parking lot. The side door slid open and a big man with broad shoulders and a scarred face leaped out, laser carbine clutched in his hands.

Marcus Steele. Hell Squad's leader.

Another man followed, with an intense face and a shaved head. He was a mix of races, but from the shade of his dark skin, she'd guess one of his parents was black. The predatory way he moved told her he knew how to fight, and that you didn't want to meet him on the battlefield and be on opposing teams.

Two more people exited the Hawk. A man and a woman. Sniper, by the looks of the lanky man's long-range rifle, and a dark-haired woman who looked like she ate nails for breakfast, lunch and dinner.

Then a young man leaped out. The sun glinted

off his blond hair and eager face. She knew Hell Squad had lost one of their team to the raptors about a month back. She guessed this green kid was their replacement.

Then her heart leaped. *Cruz.*

He landed beside Marcus and was saying something, even as his gaze scanned the area around them.

Okay, so the way the man was put together worked for her. No harm in looking. He was shorter and leaner than his teammates, although by no means soft. She wished she could see through his black body armor. Santha bet the view beneath would be just as fine as his handsome face. And oh boy, that was a hell of a face.

Then Santha thought of Kareena. Her sister had been so beautiful and full of life. And now she was no longer here to tease Santha about her interest in handsome men.

Santha moved the binoculars away from Hell Squad.

She was out here to get revenge for Kareena. Not ogle Cruz Ramos.

Then Santha caught movement about a kilometer from Hell Squad's landing spot. *Raptors.* Crouched amongst the ruins of a small office building.

She zoomed back to the Hell Squad. They were moving now, led by the sniper and the tough-looking woman. The team moved together like a well-oiled machine, something she knew took practice. She'd been like that with her team. A pang hit her as she thought of the men and women who'd been like family to her. Now all dead.

Then she noted where Hell Squad were headed. Toward the raptors.

She swung back to the aliens, and spied the small dish set up near the top of their hiding place. She knew what it was. A jammer. It would jam the feed from the drones Hell Squad used to locate the enemy.

Hell Squad were moving right into a raptor ambush.

Dammit. Her heart kicked against her ribs.

Standing, she slung her crossbow over her shoulder, then grabbed the line she had tied to the top of the building. With her Kevlar gloves on, she simply gripped the rope and swung off the side of the building in a wide arc, sliding down to the ground.

Her feet hit concrete and she bent to absorb the impact.

A half-second later, she was sprinting for her bike.

***

Cruz Ramos kicked his boot through some rubble on the street. Under the pile was a small, tattered teddy bear.

He crouched and picked up the toy. He wondered what had happened to the child who'd owned it. Cruz looked up and scanned the empty houses. Some splintered doors stood open, the roofs damaged, windows broken, the walls smoke stained. Other homes looked perfectly normal, like a happy family still lived inside.

He wanted to believe the child had gotten away, maybe made it to Blue Mountain Base. But inside, Cruz felt a growing numbness. He dropped the toy. He knew what had happened to the kid who'd loved the stupid bear.

Sometimes he wondered why the hell he and the squad bothered. Fighting off the empty, dark feeling, he focused on the rest of his team.

Marcus was nearby, alert for anything that might crop up, and murmuring to the team's communications officer through his comms device. He was a hell of a team leader, always had a plan B when shit hit…which it always did. Hell Squad got the best missions.

In his own earpiece, Cruz heard their comms officer, Elle, laugh at something Marcus said. Cruz almost smiled. She did a hell of a job providing their intel…and she was also officially the love of Marcus' life. Cruz shook his head. He'd watched the two of them dance around their feelings for months. He would never have guessed slim, classy Elle—former society girl—and rough, tough, battle-hardened Marcus Steele would be a match made in heaven. But they fit.

The team's sniper walked past Cruz, followed by Hell Squad's female team member. For once, Claudia and Shaw weren't bickering. A minor miracle. They were both quiet and focused.

"So, we gonna whip some raptor butt?"

The voice from beside him made Cruz roll his eyes. "Kid, you want to keep your voice down."

A clearing throat. "Right."

Sam Jenkins was on a trial run to fill the empty slot on Hell Squad. The best soldiers were already on the squads, so the pickings were slim for replacements. As far as Cruz could tell, Sam was young, eager, but with limited experience. He'd been in the United Coalition Military Academy when the invasion had hit. His shininess would either wear off real quick and he'd quit, or he'd get himself killed.

Cruz glanced at Gabe, who was just a little behind them. He had a way of moving that was spooky and completely silent. He could disappear into shadows in the blink of an eye. His brother had been almost as good.

Jesus, Zeke. Whenever Cruz thought of their fallen teammate, he felt a flood of anger. But even that flash of emotion faded quickly. Consumed by the growing deadness inside that he couldn't seem to shake.

Death. Destruction. Blood and fighting.

Sometimes, he couldn't remember what he was fighting for anymore.

Something tingled along Cruz's senses. He slowed, turning his head to study the surrounding buildings. Nothing moved. Even the air was still.

He stopped and turned in a slow circle.

Marcus held up a closed fist. The team halted.

"Cruz?" Marcus murmured.

Cruz couldn't see or hear anything that should

have set off his internal alarm. "I don't know, *amigo*." But something was wrong.

"Marcus?" Elle's voice. "We've lost the drone feed. I can't see you guys or what's around you."

As Marcus cursed, Cruz's gut cramped. Yeah, something was really off.

Then he heard a noise. Cruz spun, and straight ahead, speeding toward them, was a slim figure in black. Her black hair flew out behind her and he saw the tip of her crossbow over her shoulder.

Santha. Everything in him flared to life.

Her sleek, black bike was electric and made no sound. Perfect for sneaking around the city.

As she got closer, he saw her face, watched her wave one arm at them madly.

Shit. "Everyone, take cover!" he yelled.

Seconds later, raptors streamed out of a building ahead. Their weapons made a distinctive noise as they fired. Dark-green ooze splattered the road in front of the team. It sizzled and hissed as it ate through the asphalt.

He knew the damned stuff burned and paralyzed. He ducked in behind an abandoned car. *Madre de dios*, another thirty seconds and they would have walked right into the raptor cluster fuck.

Looked like the aliens had fully recovered their communications and were out for some payback.

Hell Squad dived for cover. Cruz watched Santha coax more speed from her bike. Even with the gunfire, she rode straight, heading for him.

She skidded the bike in a tight turn and came to

a stop beside him. "Ambush. Had to warn you."

With a nod, he sprung to his feet and leaped on the back of bike.

She swiveled. "What the hell are—?"

"Ride."

She did. They raced through the raptors. Cruz aimed his carbine and pulled out his secondary weapon, a smaller laser pistol. He fired both weapons, taking down any raptor in range.

Santha turned the bike again and Cruz held on his with knees. They moved through the aliens again and Cruz kept firing. His team members were firing as well.

He and Santha did another loop. She anticipated his needs, slowing down, speeding up, tuning to avoid the raptor gunfire. Even in the middle of hell, he took a second to appreciate her lean body pressed back against him.

Then he saw a huge raptor, over seven feet tall, dragging Sam across the ground by his ankle. The young soldier was struggling and had lost his weapon.

Dammit. "Slow down!"

She did and Cruz leaped off the bike.

He unloaded his carbine into the raptor. It took a rain of laser fire, but the giant raptor finally tumbled to the ground like a felled tree.

Sam lay writhing, his right leg bent at an odd angle. Cruz yanked the kid up and hefted Sam over his shoulder. The kid probably weighed more than Cruz, but the slim-line exoskeleton in Cruz's armor helped him lift heavy loads. He ran for cover.

Behind an overturned minivan, he set Sam down. The kid was moaning, his eyes wide and jittery. "T-thanks, Cruz."

Claudia appeared. "He okay?"

"Leg's broken."

"I'll take a look."

The team didn't have a field medic, but they all had basic training. As Claudia splinted Sam's leg, Cruz ducked out of cover to check on Santha.

She was still on the bike, riding toward the remaining raptors. She held something in her hand.

He frowned, and then, when he realized what it was, he grinned. Damn, she was his kind of woman, a queen among warriors.

She tossed the grenade into a group of raptors then made a tight turn on the bike. She rode back, standing up to make a small jump over some rubble. Behind her, the grenade exploded, flames reaching into the sky. The screams and grunts of wounded and dying raptors filled the air.

"They're retreating." Marcus' gravelly voice came through Cruz's earpiece.

The last of the raptors slipped away through the ruins in full retreat. Warily, gun up, Cruz walked into the middle of the street.

Santha stopped her bike with a skid. The rest of Hell Squad came out of cover.

"Thanks for the warning and the help," Marcus said.

She nodded. "You should get going. Their usual MO is to come in with a larger force, and a pack of canids."

Cruz grimaced. He hated canids. The alien hunting dogs were vicious and relentless.

Marcus cursed. "We were supposed to check for some survivors our drones spotted in a school about a block from here."

Santha shook her head. "They left three days ago. Don't know where they are now."

Marcus nodded. "Thanks." He touched his ear. "Elle, can you send a Hawk our way and have the doc meet us back at base? Jenkins is injured." Marcus glanced at his team. "Hell Squad, let's move out. Gabe, carry Sam."

The armor's exoskeleton meant that carrying a team member, even for several hours, wasn't hard, but Cruz knew Gabe probably didn't need the help of the exoskeleton.

Cruz stepped close to Santha. "Come with us."

Another shake of her head.

He moved closer until his body was just a whisper from hers. He smelled her—sweat and a fragrant woody scent. "Come back to base. There's a place for you there."

"I'm not leaving."

Dammit. Cruz barely resisted the urge to kick something. He hated the idea of her out here, alone. "Why not?"

Her green eyes flashed. "I have work to do."

He leaned closer and saw her stiffen. "Don't you get lonely?" he asked quietly.

"You think being with a bunch of strangers will help with that?" She tilted her head. "You're with people all the time and you're still lonely."

Cruz felt his muscles tense. He stepped back. "What are you going to do?"

She revved the bike. "Keep fighting."

With frustration like a noose around his neck, he forced himself to nod. "Don't get yourself killed."

She flashed him a smile. The first he'd ever seen from her. "Sure thing, soldier."

She gunned the bike and shot away.

Cruz watched her disappear from sight. Yeah, she was right. Even surrounded by his team, he was lonely as hell.

Institute of Historic Preservation, refuses to back her expedition. Left with no choice, Eos must trust the most notorious treasure hunter in the galaxy, a man she finds infuriating, annoying and far too tempting.

Dathan Phoenix can sniff out relics at a stellar mile. With his brothers by his side, he takes the adventures that suit him and refuses to become a lazy, bitter failure like their father. When the gorgeous Eos Rai comes looking to hire him, he knows she's trouble, but he's lured into a hunt that turns into a wild and dangerous adventure. As Eos and Dathan are pushed to their limits, they discover treasure isn't the only thing they're drawn to…but how will their desire survive when Dathan demands the *Mona Lisa* as his payment?

The Phoenix Adventures

At Star's End
In the Devil's Nebula
On a Rogue Planet
Beneath a Trojan Moon
Beyond Galaxy's Edge
On a Cyborg Planet

Also by Anna Hackett

Hell Squad

Marcus

Cruz

Gabe

Reed

The Anomaly Series

Time Thief

Mind Raider

Soul Stealer

Salvation

Perma Series

Winter Fusion

The WindKeepers Series

Wind Kissed, Fire Bound

Taken by the South Wind

Tempting the West Wind

Defying the North Wind

Claiming the East Wind

Standalone Titles

Savage Dragon

Hunter's Surrender

One Night with the Wolf

Anthologies

A Galactic Holiday

Moonlight (UK only)

Vampire Hunter (UK only)

Awakening the Dragon (UK Only)

About the Author

I'm passionate about ***action romance***. I love stories that combine the thrill of falling in love with the excitement of action, danger and adventure. I'm a sucker for that moment when the team is walking in slow motion, shoulder-to-shoulder heading off into battle. I write about people overcoming unbeatable odds and achieving seemingly impossible goals. I like to believe it's possible for all of us to do the same.

My books are mixture of action, adventure and sexy romance and they're recommended for anyone who enjoys fast-paced stories where the boy wins the girl at the end (or sometimes the girl wins the boy!)

For release dates, action romance info, free books, and other fun stuff, sign up for the latest news here:

Website: AnnaHackettBooks.com

Printed in Great Britain
by Amazon

86721612R00123